"Your sister begged me to make sure Libby stays with us."

"*Us?*" Travis gave Kit a cautious half smile that reminded her so much of when they'd been kids. Back when it had taken her a minute to breathe after he'd shyly confessed his attraction for her.

"Well..." She licked her lips. "She said *us*, you and me together, but I'm sure she meant me in the short-term, then you for the long-term."

"Sure."

"Because otherwise, she would've meant us as a couple, only Marlene was never really the matchmaking type. Besides, she knew I'm happy with Levi."

"Right. And that I'm not the relationship type."

"Of course." Travis had stopped at an intersection, and though the cars whizzed along the paved highway they faced, flooding the truck's cab with a much-needed breeze, for Kit, the temperature under Travis's hooded gaze blazed as hot as ever.

"So what do you want, Travis?"

Dear Reader,

What's more fun than a summer fling? Late-night walks, holding hands to the accompaniment of moonlight and crickets—or mosquitoes if you're in my neck of the woods! Luckily for Kit and Travis, they live in a fictional Arkansas town, where there are no whiny bugs—just romance.

Back before I became old and married, summer romances were always my favorite. I was a "Bandie," meaning every summer I packed up my clarinet and headed off to the University of Arkansas, Fayetteville campus for band camp. Sure, we were supposed to be practicing our instruments, but what we mostly got practice on was scoping new guys!

The best part of camp was always the dance held at week's end. Sure, it was sad, knowing you'd soon say goodbye to all your new friends, but the poignancy of the moment seemed to add urgency, accelerating relationships that ordinarily might take all year. After a few sweet kisses, it was over, save for letter writing that eventually faded along with summer's heat.

Travis and Kit first met the summer he was seventeen and she was sixteen. Now they're all grown-up and it's summer again. Will things work out any better for them this time? Hmm... Beats me. You'll have to read the book to find out!

Happy reading,

Laura Marie ;-)

Daddy Daycare

LAURA MARIE ALTOM

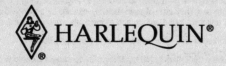

HARLEQUIN®

TORONTO • NEW YORK • LONDON
AMSTERDAM • PARIS • SYDNEY • HAMBURG
STOCKHOLM • ATHENS • TOKYO • MILAN • MADRID
PRAGUE • WARSAW • BUDAPEST • AUCKLAND

ISBN-13: 978-0-373-75136-5
ISBN-10: 0-373-75136-2

DADDY DAYCARE

www.eHarlequin.com

Printed in U.S.A.

ABOUT THE AUTHOR

After college (Go Hogs!), bestselling, award-winning author Laura Marie Altom did a brief stint as an interior designer before becoming a stay-at-home mom to boy/girl twins. Always an avid romance reader, she knew it was time to try her hand at writing when she found herself replotting the afternoon soaps.

When not immersed in her next story, Laura enjoys an almost glamorous lifestyle of zipping around in a convertible while trying to keep her dog from leaping out, and constantly striving to reach the bottom of the laundry basket—a feat she may never accomplish! For real fun, Laura is content to read, do needlepoint and cuddle with her kids and handsome hubby.

Laura loves hearing from readers at either P.O. Box 2074, Tulsa, OK 74101, or e-mail: BaliPalm@aol.com. Or check out lauramariealtom.com.

Books by Laura Marie Altom

HARLEQUIN AMERICAN ROMANCE

1028—BABIES AND BADGES
1043—SANTA BABY
1074—TEMPORARY DAD
1086—SAVING JOE*
1099—MARRYING THE MARSHAL*
1110—HIS BABY BONUS*
1123—TO CATCH A HUSBAND*

*U.S. Marshals

For Betty Anne Miller and Dixie Miller—
There aren't enough words to describe how thankful
I am to you two for being such great temp
moms to my Hannah! (Not to mention such
super friends to me!) We wouldn't have made it
through middle school without you!

Chapter One

"Ouch," Kit Wells said with a whimper, rubbing the back of her throbbing head. Never had she known such pain.

Well...at least physical pain. The emotional pain of losing her best friend in a freak car accident—that was still as crushing as it had been yesterday when Marlene died in her arms.

Focusing on the task at hand, which was fishing one of her best gold earrings out from under CEO Travis Callahan's desk, she snatched the errant piece of jewelry, then backed up, only to slam the top of her head when she rose too early.

She was still on the floor when the office's door creaked open. Between the stars flashing before her eyes and the ball-and-claw feet of navy leather wing chairs she spied a pair of obviously expensive black, highly polished wingtip shoes. Wearing those were long, long legs encased in creased black dress pants. As her gaze traveled up, she saw a matching black jacket, starched white shirt and red-striped power tie. After a quick gulp, Kit summoned the courage to finish her visual sweep. Precision-cut short dark hair, chiseled features and eyes the shade of fresh-ground coffee made it official—the man was gorgeous. Even better than thirteen years earlier, when he'd last visited her hometown of IdaBelle Falls.

"Um, hi," she said with a faint smile. "Remember me? I'm Kit. The girl you, um…well, *you know,* under your grandmother's backyard mulberry tree." Though she felt like conking herself on her already swimming head for blurting that bit of inane history—despite that to date, his kisses, among other things, were still some of her best in memory—Kit yanked down the hem of her brown prairie-style skirt, then tried scrambling to her feet. In fact, Travis's kisses had been so dreamy, his technique had even topped that of Brad Foley, the B-movie actor who'd finished the job of demolishing what had been left of Kit's heart after Travis left town. But that was a long story best forgotten.

As of late, she'd settled into a nice, safe engagement with local hardware store owner Levi Petty. What Levi lacked in animal magnetism and flash, he more than made up for in good old-fashioned family values and stability.

"Need help?" She looked up to see Travis's proffered hand, which she took, only to regret it. No way were her sparks for him as intense as when she'd been a gangly teen and he'd been equally handsome.

Both of which were entirely inappropriate observations considering the task she'd flown all the way from IdaBelle Falls to downtown Chicago to do.

"Um, please," she said, releasing him the instant she was back on her sturdy sandals. Never had she wished she was more the polished sophisticate like all the other women she'd seen in the building, but since she was only going to be here long enough to tell Travis her news, then be out on an afternoon flight, it really hadn't made sense to blow much-needed cash on some swanky outfit she'd wear only once. She really shouldn't have spent the money to come here. But when her friend Alex, who was on the IdaBelle Falls police force, said they'd intended to tell Travis the news over the phone, out of love for his sister Kit had begged Mitch to let her break the news herself.

"Thanks," she said, brushing at her behind, then adjusting her fitted brown-and-gold shirt before moving up to secure her disastrous head full of curly dark hair, which had sprung free of its clip.

"You're welcome. And yes, I remember you and the mulberry tree. My sister speaks of you often—at least when she's not barraging me with amazing baby feats performed by my adorable niece." The smile he flashed would've been perfect, only it didn't quite reach his eyes. And as far as Kit knew, through Marlene, Travis hadn't cracked a genuine smile since he'd taken this CEO gig.

At the mention of Travis's sister—Kit's longtime best friend—bone-deep sorrow reclaimed her. Yes, telling Travis in person about Marlene's death was the right thing to do but also agonizingly hard.

"Not to be rude," he asked, "but would you mind letting me in on the gag my sister no doubt put you up to that's led to you being camped out in my office?"

Tears stung her eyes, but Kit stoically blinked them away. Now was not the time for more of her own mourning. She had to be strong. Travis would need her, as would his adorable baby niece, Libby.

"Simple," Kit said, forcing a deep breath. "We need to talk. And…" She fumbled her hands at her waist. "Well, it's one of those conversations best held in person."

"Sure," he said, scratching his head. "Makes perfect sense." Glancing around as if he expected someone else to pop out at any moment yelling *Surprise!* he asked, "So? Where is she?"

"Marlene?" Kit's heart raced and her mouth went dry. She couldn't tell him his sister was dead like this. Not while standing around his office, shooting the breeze. Forcing a half smile, she replied, "She's not here. How about we sit, then I'll tell you all about her."

"Sure," he said, eyeing her as if she were a three-headed alien fresh off the ship from Mars. "But first I need to take care of business." He gestured toward a private bath she hadn't before noticed.

"Sure." Reddening from the coral-painted tips of her toes to the top of her head, Kit stumbled into the nearest chair. "I'll, uh, wait."

"Thanks. That'd be great."

WITH THE RESTROOM DOOR closed, for the first time since grasping Kit's hand, Travis Callahan breathed.

On the outside he might seem as if he had life by the balls—at least he hoped that was how he came across—but on the inside it was a whole different beast. Not that he wasn't one hundred percent at the top of his game, but the international electronics world kept changing. Growing evermore high-staked. Though he happened to be damned good at what he did—supervising the design and manufacture of an array of electronics ranging from flat-panel TVs to personal MP3 players—that didn't mean Travis liked his job.

What he did, in the simplest of terms, was done out of respect for the paternal grandparents who'd raised him. The company had been his grandfather's baby since a time when phonographs had been all the rage. So when, on his deathbed, Mitchell Callahan handed the reins to Travis days before his twenty-second birthday, what else could he have done but graciously accept, then carry on the family tradition? Up until five minutes ago he'd been mindlessly numb doing just that. Which was why being faced with this fresh-faced, pretty blast from his past had caught him off guard. Reminded him of secret hopes and dreams best forgotten.

After taking care of business, then washing and drying his hands, he stood at the counter for ten long seconds, staring at himself in the mirror. Maybe, with any luck, when he stepped outside that door, his security team would've gotten their heads out of their behinds enough to realize the woman who looked better dressed for a relaxed day at the county fair didn't belong at Rose Industries.

Forcing a deep breath, he squared his shoulders, knowing most folks found his six-three height intimidating. Why, he didn't pretend to know, but that's how he wanted Kit to feel—intimidated. Because, dammit, that's what she'd done to him. He'd once felt comfortable around not only her but other women, like Natalie—the college coed he'd fully planned to marry after getting out of Notre Dame. But then he'd caught her in bed graduation night with his supposed best friend and frat brother. Ever since, he'd sworn off women in favor of business. Oh, sure, he enjoyed long-legged companionship as much as the next guy—assuming she left his Lakeshore Drive penthouse long before sunrise—but for the most part he preferred avoiding the fairer sex altogether.

"Better?" she asked when he emerged from the bathroom.

He cast her a half grin before landing behind his antique mahogany desk. Oddly enough, that one small step went a long way toward regaining the control that'd only briefly been lost in his head. Suddenly Travis did feel better. In control.

He cleared his throat. "It's been great catching up, but as you can see—" he gestured to the foot-high stack of paperwork threatening to topple "—I've got a full plate. So, what's the problem? My sister need more shopping cash or lost her ATM card? Where is she, by the way?"

Even though it'd been over a decade since Travis had last seen Kit, her grass-green eyes were still piercing, her smile still pretty—at least until it faded like the sun blanketed by clouds. She then began fidgeting, rummaging through a purse that looked more like a small picnic basket until she found a tissue. Next came a slight hiccup before a full-force gale leading to a teary monsoon.

"Hey, whoa…" he said, walking out from behind his desk to slip his arm around her—in a strictly brotherly way. Nothing remotely like the way he used to hold her all those years ago. Not sure what else to do, he gave her a few awkward pats. "I'm, uh, sure everything's going to be okay."

"No," she said, "not ever. Oh, Travis. Marlene, she's—"

Travis's intercom buzzed. "Mr. Callahan, Steve Ford from Kline and Foster is holding on line three. He says it's urgent."

Crap. Torn between the sobbing beauty in front of him and the make-or-break deal awaiting him on the phone, Travis weighed his options. Door number one: do the decent thing and help his sister's gal pal through whatever crisis had her down. No doubt boyfriend or money trouble. Temporarily frustrating but ultimately fixable. Door number two: get the kinks worked out of a merger he'd been setting up for close to a year that would net Rose Industries a cool fifty million.

"Sorry…" he said to the woman who might as well have been from another lifetime. One in which he hadn't been the jaded, world-weary soul he was today. "I've got to take this call."

She nodded and sniffled.

He gave her back another pat.

Five minutes later, back behind his desk, he hung up the phone. "You any better?"

"No," she said, even though she'd nodded.

"Well, if it's love that's got you down, no doubt Marlene and her big mouth have let you in on the fact that I don't get it—the whole institution—so I won't be of much help to you there. However, if you've got creditors on your back, I'd be happy to see what I can do."

"Th-thank you," she said, "but neither of those scenarios apply. I wish they did, but—"

"Mr. Callahan, Helena Liatos with Vamvakidis Shipping is on line two. She says it's urgent."

"Go ahead," his sister's friend said. "The news I have will wait. Your sister's already dead."

He'd been on the line a good two minutes when he said to the woman Kit presumed was Helena, "I'm going to transfer you to my money man for your answer." Ten seconds later, his intense dark gaze focused on her, he asked, "What did you say?"

"I'm sorry, Travis. I'd planned to break it to you gently, but—"

"Look…" He shook his head. "I know I haven't visited Marlie like I should. And as for you, well, what we shared was amazing. But I really don't see how that gives the two of you the right to barge in here, mucking up my day with sick practical jokes when—"

"Trust me," she said, swallowing hard. "This is no joke. I'm sorry, Travis. So very sorry. But your sister's dead."

"What?" Travis lurched forward in his chair. Surely he hadn't heard Kit right? But the grim set of her once-smiling mouth had him thinking otherwise. She dug in her picnic basket of a purse again and pulled out a press clipping, which she handed to him. Under a heading that read "Fiery Crash Destroys Young Family" were two photos. One of a mangled car, the other the most recent photo Marlene had had taken of Libby when a traveling photographer had been at the Hartsville Wal-Mart four weeks ago. Travis knew when it'd been taken because Marlie had sent him a copy. Logically, he thought, if she was still around to send pictures, making him feel guilty about already having missed so much of Libby's small life, then this visit from Kit was no doubt another ploy to get him to—

"It was sudden," Kit said. "I was babysitting and she and Gary were driving home from Joe's Tavern— you know, that old two-step place out on Highway 14? Marlene loves—loved—to dance. Anyway, Gary hadn't had a drop to drink all night, but you know how foggy it gets on Bald Mountain. A truck driver cut that sharp curve by the abandoned gas station. G-Gary—he died instantly. But Marlene hung on long enough to—"

"No," Travis said with a firm shake of his head. Pushing his chair back, he stood. Paced before the stunning floor-to-ceiling view of glistening Lake Michigan. It was a breezy day and the shoreline was alive with sailboats. Travis had always wanted to learn to sail—not that he didn't already know the basics from back when he'd taken lessons as a kid, but he now wanted to know the exhilarating sport inside and out. Just hadn't yet had the time. Maybe when Marlene finally moved back home to Chicago they could pick a boat together. Something with a safe spot for Libby and landlubber Gary, who was a great guy.

G-Gary—he died instantly. But Marlene hung on long enough to—

Travis pressed the heels of his hands to stinging eyes.

The intercom buzzed. "Mr. Callahan, Helena Liatos is back on line two. She says it's crucial that you—"

"Hold all my calls," Travis barked into the system's microphone.

Lips pressed tight, he shook his head. "I just talked to Marlie—what?—last week? So this can't be right," he said in reference to the press clip's date. He tapped it. "I remember because she'd been yapping at me about coming down to Arkansas for the Fourth of July, but with this merger and everything I—"

"At the time of her death, police were going to call

you, but I thought it'd be better—kinder—to tell you like this. Face-to-face. She loved you very much."

"Our grandparents always wanted her to come back. Her place was here."

"She always said she had no head for business. You have to know she loved Gary—and her life in IdaBelle Falls—very much. She was happy. Working alongside you at Rose Industries wasn't for her."

"Nice she had a choice," he thundered, turning to slam his fist on the desk. Out of a sense of duty he'd taken over the business, while, after inheriting their maternal grandmother's place two years after graduating from Michigan State, Marlie had run off to Arkansas to play on the farm. He'd told her he didn't mind, but deep inside he'd wanted her here. He'd missed indulging her rebellious streak since her every whim had shown him glimpses of what a less-structured life might be like. Her free spirit had filled him with just enough crazy urges to run off to Tahiti to make him see how asinine such a step would be. "Where does she think the money comes from to fund her laid-back country lifestyle?"

"I know you're upset," Kit said, "but that doesn't give you the right to put her down. And, for the record, she never spent a dime of the money you sent her—well, not after we had the initial investment we needed to get the daycares rolling."

"She's not dead."

She rose, tried awkwardly to slip her arms around

him, but Travis shrugged her away before resuming his pace across the large room.

"This isn't happening," he said.

"I know. I mean, I know how you must feel. I was pretty out of it myself for a while. But there was Libby to consider, and—"

"Where is she? How is she?" he asked, staring out the windows. "My niece."

"She's fine. With Gary's parents, but—"

Turning, Travis strode across the office to throw open the door. To his secretary he said, "Mrs. Holmes, please see if the corporate jet is available."

Chapter Two

Oppressive July heat shimmered off a runway barely long enough to accommodate the plane. The terminal consisted of what was essentially a fancy shed boasting a sign that read IdaBelle Falls, USA. Rolling green hills lined with forest flattened into valleys of prime grazing pastures. Travis had been to IdaBelle Falls once since his sister up and moved to their maternal grandmother's home. While her inheriting it hadn't been a surprise, her leaving Chicago to live there had.

Though the gentleman that'd been drummed into Travis since he'd been a small boy offered his hand to help Kit down the plane's short, steep flight of stairs, his mind was on matters other than how small and fragile her fingers felt in his. As Marlie's best friend, Kit must be hurting. But part of his problem was how could he be of comfort to her when a large part of him still didn't believe it was true—that his sister was really gone?

Marlene always had been trying to get him to come for a visit. So he could see how her "kinder, gentler way of life" was presumably so much better than his. She'd wanted him to be "real." One thing he'd never gotten her to understand was his all-too real sense of duty to keep the family business in the family. More times than he could count, she'd urged him to cash out and spend the rest of his life having fun. Pursuing his own dreams—whatever they may be—not his grandfather's. Sounded good in theory, but responsibility was so deeply ingrained in Travis, how was he supposed to turn beach bum now? Or, for that matter, take up a slower paced life here in the town Marlene had so loved?

Just thinking her name sent a pang ripping through him.

She can't be gone, he thought, using every shred of willpower to keep his composure.

He'd watched out for her since they'd been kids. Their chronically battling folks had died young. Their adventure-seeking dad broke his neck while hang gliding off Baja. Travis had been thirteen. Marlie ten. Their mom died three years later from a drug overdose backstage at some Goth concert she'd been attending with her latest boyfriend, who had been twenty years her junior. Yes, their parents' deaths had been rough. But as cold as it might seem, since he and Marlie essentially had been raised by their paternal grandparents and an endless succession of servants, they hadn't missed their parents all that much.

They'd had each other. Yeah, a lot of times Marlene had been a pain in Travis's ass, but most times she'd been a cute mascot he and his friends had enjoyed having around.

"There's Levi," Kit said, quickening her pace to the tall, lean man standing, arms crossed, beside a mud-splattered red pickup.

Travis inwardly groaned. Levi was Kit's fiancé. During the hour-long flight, Travis had learned the apparently perfect man owned the town's only hardware/lumber store and had helped renovate the big red barn Marlie and Kit purchased to house the latest of their six daycares, which were in neighboring small towns. Kit traveled to each center, acting in a managerial position and occasionally filling in as needed while Marlene had done the books.

Travis couldn't fathom why, but it irked him seeing Levi hold Kit proprietarily close, planting a brief kiss on her lips before settling in for a long hug.

Kit had tried giving Travis a hug back in his office, but he'd sidestepped the affection. Now, alone on a hot runway that reeked of jet fuel, Travis could've very much used a hug. So far from his desk, he didn't feel like a powerful CEO but like the kid who'd arrived at this same airport well over a decade earlier, about to meet his maternal grandmother for only the second time.

He remembered his grandmother as a warm, simple woman. Her home a barely standing two-story, three-bedroom hodgepodge of additions. A day into his and Marlie's visit, their grandmother had introduced them to the neighbor girl, Kit. From that moment on he'd been smitten by the long-legged brunette's many charms.

For an endless summer he'd been part of the small town community. Felt as if he'd genuinely belonged.

If he were brutally honest, Kit had been his first love. Hell, maybe his only real love. And his feelings hadn't been about the physical—the making love—that had drawn him to her. Everything about her from her cute accent to her casual clothes to her unabashed belly laughs had been miles from his stuffy, painfully polite upbringing. Her carefree spirit had reeled him in from her first friendly hello.

On a sweltering August Sunday, at this same airport, saying goodbye to Kit and her uncluttered way of life had been one of the hardest things he'd ever done. Sure, they'd promised to write, but after a couple letters apiece, as much as he'd still cared for her, the guys at his private school had ribbed him mercilessly for his summer fling with an *Arkie*. And so, bowing to peer pressure—something that still deeply shamed him—he'd put Kit, their magical summer and an unobtainable longing to be part of a real family from his mind.

Until now, when Kit was the only tangible link to anything he'd once known. Sure, there was Libby, but she barely knew him. And yet, from this moment on, due to a tragic twist of fate, he was to be her father. *Father.* How could he be good for Libby when half the time he wasn't all that sure he was doing such a hot job raising himself?

"Hey," said Levi, dressed in faded jeans, a red T-shirt and white Razorbacks cap. He held out his calloused hand for Travis to shake. "You must be that hotshot CEO brother Marlene was all the time talking about."

Travis winced. Was that how his sister saw him?

With a partial smile, Travis returned the man's handshake.

"Sorry about Marlene and Gary," Levi said, taking Travis's lone black bag and setting it in the truck's bed. "They were a great couple. Everyone loved them."

Travis's throat tightened.

Thankfully, after a few awkward moments of silence, Kit said, "Well, guess we should get going."

"Yeah." Levi opened his door. "I left old Ben in charge, and you know how he is about getting so wrapped up in his afternoon soaps that he forgets we even have customers."

On the way to the passenger side of Kit's fiancé's pickup, Travis asked the obvious. "Why not get rid of the TV? Or old Ben?"

"Simple," Levi said, climbing behind the wheel. "The women who come in watch TV while their husbands shop, and I give them popcorn popped with the special coconut oil I sell. Since adding the TV and snacks, plus a few shelves of girlie knickknacks, my overall sales have gone up thirty percent."

"Sweet," Travis said, removing his suffocating

suit jacket and rolling up his sleeves before climbing into the too-small cab beside Kit.

"Where to first?" Levi asked.

Kit said, "Travis wants to see Libby."

"You're evidently a very brave or a very stupid man," Levi said, starting the truck, then putting it into gear.

"How's that?" Travis loosened his tie, wishing he'd had Mrs. Holmes look into a rental limo and driver from Little Rock. Sitting this close to Kit wasn't good. Even sweaty, she smelled intriguing. Earthy. Like the meadow where she'd taken him on a surprise picnic the afternoon after the night they'd first kissed.

Oblivious to his discomfort, Levi and Kit shared a laugh.

Kit patted Travis's left thigh, causing still more inadvertent grief. "In meeting Gary's parents—most especially his mother—you're in for a *real* treat."

"LIKE HELL YOU'RE TAKING my only granddaughter one foot outside city limits." Beulah Redding, Marlene's mother-in-law, was indeed turning out to be a treat. Five-eight and weighing a good three hundred pounds, she had a huge mass of Dolly Parton-style blond curls and a vast collection of windmills of every conceivable shape and size, including three real ones on the expansive front lawn and five out back. All that aside, the woman's house was immaculate, as was six-month-old Libby, who was dressed in a cute pink jumper with her dark curls smelling of a recent washing and her skin scented with that baby-pink lotion Marlene had constantly been rubbing all over her.

"Be reasonable," Travis said, helping himself to a seat on a blue velveteen sofa in the peach-colored room. "According to my sister and your son's will, which Marlene had sent me a copy of for safekeeping in the event of…well, you know…" Travis couldn't even bring himself to yet say the words. "Anyway, in the event we now find ourselves in, Marlene specifically named me as Libby's guardian."

Beulah switched off *Jerry Springer,* then settled into the recliner opposite the sofa. Kit, who sat on a brown floral sofa on the opposite wall beside a gurgling windmill fountain, looked every bit as uncomfortable as Travis felt. Lucky Levi had been dropped off at his store to supervise old Ben.

"I don't care what the will says," Beulah said, smacking the copy she'd been carrying around ever since plopping Libby into one of those baby activity seats bursting with knobs and squeakies for tiny fingers to explore, "I know in my heart he wished for me and his father to be Libby's guardians. That way she can be raised right here with us. Learning our values—not *your* big city ways."

As if he were negotiating a difficult business arrangement, Travis counted to ten in his head, then calmly cast Beulah the same always-in-control smile he'd used for his last magazine cover shoot. "While I appreciate your unique interpretation of the will's *true* intent, as well as your fine home, you must know

I can give Libby things—show her things—that would never be possible here in IdaBelle Falls. The Eiffel Tower. The Great Pyramids. Broadway."

Beulah notched her chin higher. "I can show her how to can my prizewinning bread-and-butter pickles. How not to get snookered when buying windmills off of eBay."

Travis cleared his throat. "That's all well and good, but I'll provide a world-class education."

Sitting straighter, Beulah said, "You implying our teachers here in IdaBelle Falls are somehow lacking? Because if you are, you can go right back to that big city of yours and ask how many of their schools had a record thirty-five students out of a graduating class of fifty go on to college. And most all of them on scholarships, I might add."

"While that's an impressive statistic," Travis noted, fixing the woman with his best boardroom stare, "I've faxed the will to my corporate attorney, and he assures me that no matter your objections, I have the legal right to pack up Libby and take her wherever I please."

"No offense to your high-and-mighty corporate attorney, but in case you've forgotten, I'm contesting that will," Beulah fired right back with a saccharine-sweet power smile of her own. "My legal counsel filed a court order barring you from taking my granddaughter outside county lines until a judge has time to hear both sides of our dilemma. Meaning, my granddaughter will remain with me until a formal decision is made."

"Look…" Clenching his jaw and trying his damnedest to remain even-keeled when what he really wanted was to blow, Travis stood and walked the five feet to Beulah's recliner. "I have no wish to make this ugly, but apparently on her deathbed my sister told Kit that she wanted me to raise Libby. I loved my sister very much and want nothing more than to abide by her wishes."

"Oh," Beulah said, also rising to her feet. "And seeing how you loved her so much, is that why you've only seen Libby once since she was born? And that was only because Marlene and my son brought the baby to you. Libby doesn't even know you, yet I'm with her several times a week. Now, logically speaking, who do you think is best suited to care for her? Me, her loving grandmother who's already raised one child of my own? Or you, Mr. Callahan, a bachelor so selfish and concerned with his own agenda that he didn't even have time to pencil in the occasional visit to his supposedly beloved sister. And another thing—have you ever in your whole life even changed a diaper? Let alone fixed a bottle or done a load of wash? We're Libby's family. With your history, do you even know the meaning of *family?* Why, I'll bet—"

"That'll be enough," an older man said, stepping into their not-so-happy group. Extending his hand to Travis, he said, "I'm Frank Redding, by the way. I'd say it's nice to meet you, but truthfully I've had better times meeting cottonmouths."

Likewise. Travis clenched his fists along with his jaw.

Not that he'd ever come face-to-face with one of the supposedly nasty snakes, but he damn sure took offense at being compared to one of the mean little bastards. What bothered him most, though, was how much Beulah's verbal attack stung. He knew damn well what a family was. And in his heart he also knew it hadn't been selfishness keeping him away from his sister and IdaBelle Falls all these years but an uncomfortable, far deeper emotion.

Libby started to cry.

Both Travis and Beulah lunged for her, but Kit did, too, and seeing how she was closest, she won. "Listen to you, Beulah, going on about how you're an expert on family and babies, yet raising your voice right here in front of poor little Libby, who's already been through so much."

"Sorry," Beulah said. "I just…well, when I think about this stranger here, running off to Chicago with the apple of my eye, raising her with no one around but nannies, I can't stand it."

"It'll be all right," Gary's father said, putting his arm around Beulah's quaking shoulders.

Libby was still fitfully crying.

"Here's what I propose," Kit said, easing up beside Travis with the baby. He suddenly wanted to hold both girls. Libby represented his only flesh-and-blood link to his sister. And Kit, as Marlene's best friend, would always hold a special place in his—what? Had he been about to think *heart?* Because if so, that was screwy; he hardly knew the woman. He was only feeling abnormally close to her because of his sister's sudden death. Certainly not because of one hot summer he'd gotten over a long time ago. "Why not let Libby choose?"

"That's ridiculous," Beulah said with a put-upon sigh.

"Is it?" Gary's father asked, looking intrigued.

"Whose side are you on?" she asked her husband.

"Libby's," the man said. "Until the judge has his say, I think it's only fair the little gal has her own."

"Fine," Beulah said. "Hands down, I'll win. But if this showdown makes y'all feel better, so be it." She held out her arms to Kit. "Pass her over." Cradling Libby, Beulah crooned and coddled, but no amount of talk calmed her.

"My turn," Travis said a few minutes later.

"Be my guest," Beulah said. "But when she gets like this, there's no comforting her."

"I'll take my chances." Travis took Libby into his arms, then headed for the rocking chair he'd earlier spied on the glassed in, air-conditioned front porch. Comfortably seated in the chair, tears stinging his eyes, he recalled a late-night phone call he'd had with Marlie when Libby had been two months old. The baby had been going through cranky spells in the middle of the night, and Marlene had said the only way she'd found to calm her was by rocking her, rubbing the small of her back and singing the Oscar

Mayer wiener song—a ditty she'd accidentally discovered the baby enjoyed when it'd soothed her while Marlene had been up watching TV.

Humming the familiar strains, Travis clutched his niece as if his life depended on her. Hell, maybe his life *did* depend upon her. Ever since hearing of Marlene's death, he'd been so wrapped up in the logistics of getting to IdaBelle Falls and making sure Libby ended up with him that it hadn't even sunk in that his funny, opinionated, cute, talented sister was gone.

With Libby sound asleep against his chest, her slight weight and warmth bringing unfathomable comfort, Travis looked up to find Kit swiping at a few tears of her own.

"We have a winner," she softly said.

Beulah snorted. "No one told me we could use the rocking chair. Oldest baby trick in the book. He clearly cheated. But seeing how I'm a God-fearing woman, I won't be one to go back on my word. Long as you keep an eye on him, Kit, Travis's welcome to take my grandbaby to her home. But if he so much as breathes a word about heading back to Chicago…"

"THANKS FOR YOUR HELP back there," Travis said from behind the wheel of Levi's truck. Libby was buckled into her safety seat on the passenger side, leaving Kit in the middle to care for her. Travis had to admit—out of Beulah's earshot, anyway—he knew just enough to be dangerous when it came to caring for an infant.

When Marlene and Gary had named Travis as Libby's godfather, he'd taken the title seriously, but it'd never occurred to him he'd actually wind up one day becoming the girl's substitute father. In fact, the couple had often teased him that eventually, once he had kids of his own, he'd see there was more to life than business. Laughing, he'd always said, *Yeah, yeah, that day'll never come.* Yet look at him now. An instant father halfway wondering if maybe Libby *would* be better off living with her grandmother.

"Not a problem," Kit said. "I was winging it, hoping like the devil you'd remember Marlene's wiener-song trick."

"She never told Beulah?" Coming to a four-way stop on the dirt road, he cast a sideways glance at Kit. Back in the blazing heat, her skin glowed. She'd had her dark hair up all day, but sweat-dampened tendrils escaped. She'd raised her skirt above her knees, baring endless tanned legs that, on countless sweltering nights in Foster's swimming hole, she'd wrapped around him, giving him teenage hard-ons so intense they'd hurt. Then, one thing had led to another and he was burying himself deep inside her. She'd made everything better. Good. Whole.

Why had he never told her how much she'd brought to his life?

With a sharp laugh, Kit said, "To say the two didn't get along would be the understatement of the century."

"Yeah. On a few of her calls, Marlene intimated as much. Said Beulah didn't approve of her cooking."

Even as Travis had spoken, he couldn't take his eyes off the elegant column of Kit's throat. He should've told her. Maybe before returning to Chicago he would. Assuming he found the right moment or—

"Um, Travis?" She glanced at him curiously. "You forget how to use the gas pedal? I'd like to get Libby out of this heat."

"Oh, sure." He checked the intersection again and pressed the gas.

Truth be told, Kit thought, who she really wanted out of the heat was herself—only the rising temps in the truck's cab had nothing to do with Mother Nature and everything to do with the boy she'd once fancied herself in love with who'd turned into one heckuva hunk of man. Not that she found him more attractive than Levi, just that she felt an unexpected familiarity with Travis and, in the same breath, a rush of city excitement and attraction she'd thought forever gone. On many lonely nights, *wished* forever gone.

She'd worked hard to get over what her mother and friends had considered a high school crush. So hard that after graduation she'd fallen right into another impossible relationship with Brad Foley, a B-movie actor in town filming a period piece about moonshining. After being burned twice by city guys looking for a temporary good time, Kit had learned her lesson and was now glad for her long-standing engagement to a local who had no plans to leave IdaBelle Falls and had been there for her for as long as she could remember. He was her rock. Solid. Dependable. Like the big brother she'd never had—only kissable! Levi hadn't wanted to set a wedding date until he'd built a proper nest egg, which he'd promised would be soon six months ago.

Heading down the dusty road, Kit was relieved to get her thoughts back to the current matter at hand when Travis asked, "What do you make of Beulah contesting Gary and Marlene's will?"

Kit shrugged. "I don't for a second believe she'll win. Levi and I used to double date with your sister and her husband at least once a week, and as far as I knew, Gary thought his mother was sweet but smothering. Well-intentioned but hopelessly controlling."

"Think the judge will toss her case?"

"Don't know," Kit said. "I can't imagine Marlene ever wanting this. As she was dying, she begged me to make sure Libby stays with us."

"Us?" He cast her a cautious half smile that reminded her so much of when they'd been kids. Back when it had taken her a minute to breathe after he'd shyly confessed his attraction for her.

"Well…" Kit licked her lips. "She said *us,* you and me together, but I'm sure she meant me in the short term, then you for the long term."

"Sure."

"Because otherwise she would've meant us as a couple, only Marlene was never really the matchmaking type."

"No. No, she wasn't."

"Besides which, she knows I'm happy with Levi."

"Right. And that I'm not the relationship type."

"Of course." He'd braked for another stop sign, and though cars whizzed along the paved highway they faced, flooding the truck's cab with much-needed breeze, for Kit, the temperature under Travis's hooded gaze blazed as hot as ever.

His dark eyes were beseeching. As if he desperately wanted, *needed* something from her, but wasn't sure what.

So she gave him a nudge when she asked, "Beyond losing Marlene, what's hurting you, Travis?"

Chapter Three

"Excuse me?" Travis squinted at Kit, making her feel about as needed as a pesky fly. Obviously, as in her disastrous fling with Brad, she'd totally misread the current situation. Travis most likely didn't need or want for anything but a refreshing, cool shower and a light meal. Least of all, he didn't want *her,* making her feel silly and stupid and sentimental for even having asked the question. Most of all for the brief flash of wanting something from him—namely the comfort of just being near him. Of knowing that, in his own way, he'd loved his sister every bit as fiercely as she had.

"Nothing," Kit said, fussing over the lace trim on Libby's jumper. Why did she always want to fix not only things but people? Especially people who didn't need to be fixed. Travis was the embodiment of success. He was one of the top CEOs in the country. He had brains, talent and immense wealth. What could he possibly want from her?

"You as bone-tired as I am?" she asked, blaming exhaustion on her odd mood.

"Yep." He pulled onto the highway, heading toward the airport.

"Did you forget that Marlene and Gary's new house and our latest daycare are a few miles in the other direction?"

"Nope."

"Then where are you going?"

"Home."

"What do you mean *home?*" she asked, angling on the cramped seat as best she could to face him. "As in Chicago?"

"Come with me. At least for a little while. I'll need help with Libby for the first few days. Hell," he said with a swipe of his hair, "make that the first few years. I don't have a clue what I'm doing, but I'll— we'll—figure it out."

"Hello?" she said, flashing her hand in front of his deadpan gaze. "Marlene and Gary's funeral is in two days. And what about *court order* don't you understand?"

He snorted. "We'll fly back for the funeral. And my lawyer got his degree from Harvard. Beulah's no doubt got his on the Internet. Who do you think's going to win?"

Lips set in a grim line, Kit shook her head. "Not that it's any of my business, but I think you've sorely underestimated the power of your adversary."

"You can't be serious? The woman collects windmills and cans pickles. How tough a foe can she be?"

"Have you ever canned pickles in the heat of summer?"

"Can't say I've had the pleasure."

"And that seemingly derelict windmill alongside Beulah's weeping willow? It's fifteenth-century. She had it shipped over from England. Reassembled it piece by piece all on her own. Trust me, the woman's tougher than you think."

"Yeah," Travis said with a wink, "but I've got deeper pockets."

"True. But seeing how decades ago Beulah's family moved to IdaBelle Falls to start a thorough-bred cattle business, after having already made a fortune off Oklahoma oil, I wouldn't be so sure her lawyer isn't also a Harvard grad—or at the very least, Yale." Kit sent him a wink of her own, grinning at his incredulous expression.

AN HOUR LATER, AFTER Kit had changed his mind about leaving, Travis wandered through the stuffy gloom of his sister and brother-in-law's closed-up house while Kit changed Libby's diaper—she'd insisted, arguing there'd be time enough for him to take a turn—it finally hit him. Marlene was gone. She wouldn't be back to use the hairbrush set on the bathroom counter. Or to complete the to-do list tacked to the fridge door with a cookie-shaped magnet.

His sister had been fiercely proud of this place, and he tried seeing it as the hopeful fixer-upper she would've imagined instead of as the run-down wreck it truly was. Two miles outside of town, the place was, according to his sister, one of the oldest brick homes in the county.

Though the two-story, white-columned abode looked grand from the outside, on the inside the place was a cramped, shoddy lesson in how *not* to restore a historic home. Plenty of cheap paneling over crumbling plaster walls and brown shag carpet hiding scratched wood floors. In the year Marlene and Gary had lived here, the only rooms they'd tackled were Libby's pink fairy tale of a room and what Marlene called the master bedroom suite—an oasis of modern comfort in an otherwise depressing hellhole.

Travis sent Marlene thousands every month. Why hadn't she used the money to hire contractors to do the work in a timely manner? Why had she insisted she and Gary do the work themselves? Didn't make sense.

"You okay?" Kit asked him, Libby in her arms as she descended the staircase that split the entry hall into equal halves.

"Sort of," Travis said with a sigh. "The way Marlene described this place, you'd have thought it was *Gone With the Wind*'s Tara, but…" He kicked a piece of drywall at his feet.

"They were happy here," she said, glancing up at the stained-glass skylight lending the space an otherworldly bluish glow.

"If she'd wanted an old house, the mansion we grew up in would've been sufficient. Hell, aside from the servants who maintain the place for corporate retreats, it's sat empty for years."

"Ever stop to think," Kit said from the bottom of the stairs, "that it wasn't so much an old house she wanted but her *own* house? One that she and Gary worked on together."

"Whatever," Travis said, taking the baby, kissing the top of her sweet-smelling head. "I still don't get it."

"You wouldn't."

"What's that supposed to mean?" Travis asked, chasing Kit down the long, dark hall leading to the kitchen.

Yellow light from the open fridge silhouetted her before spilling into the gloom. "Think about it," she said. "Everything Marlene wanted had been handed to her by your grandparents or servants or you. But she wanted more than material things. She wanted not just to love her family and job but to create something with her own hands. To be able to sit back at the end of a long, exhausting day and think, with a satisfied smile, I did that. I made it, I painted it, I mowed it—whatever. She had to know her life mattered. That she hadn't spent her days like some pampered lap dog but as a contributing member of society." She grabbed a few items from the fridge, then slammed it shut.

"So what you're essentially saying is that Marlene felt she was in danger of wasting her life? Like me?" Travis switched on a harsh overhead light.

Kit rolled her eyes, slapping a sealed package of

bologna, then mustard, on the worn white laminate counter before taking a bread loaf from the freezer. "Libby's formula is in the third cabinet on the left. Mind opening a can while I make us a couple sandwiches? And for the record, no—Marlene never once said or even implied you were wasting your life. She just had no interest in big business. She wanted to be more hands-on."

"Whatever," Travis said, too tired to even conceive of the luxury of having a choice. What if he'd up and told his grandfather he'd had no interest in running Rose Industries? What would've happened to their thousands of worldwide employees? All of their families and *their* families? Thinking of how many lives would have been affected by such a decision made Travis sick. He kept at it day after day because he'd had no other choice. It was as if his life had been preordained to be this way. And who knew? Maybe he'd get a kick out of occasionally plastering or painting a wall, but the sad fact of the matter was that he didn't have time for anything but work. When Libby would fit into his schedule he wasn't sure. He was taking this fatherhood gig minute by minute. "Where are Libby's bottles?"

"Here," Kit said, picking up the plastic kind that used disposable liners from a basket on the counter. "It's tricky getting the liners in the first couple times, so pay attention."

"Don't," he said, his voice dangerously low.

"What?"

"Treat me like I'm ignorant. I have spent time with Marlene and Libby."

"Sorry," Kit said. "It wasn't my intention. I just wanted to share a few helpful pointers. You forget—while your business is wheeling and dealing, mine involves a little managing and a lot of hugs."

The doorbell rang.

They both looked to the entry hall, but it was Kit who ultimately bustled off to answer the door.

Travis had been on the verge of telling Little Miss Know-It-All to take her advice elsewhere, but then she'd added that bit about hugs and stolen his fire. He could use a hug from Kit right about now. Even back when they'd been teens she'd always known the perfect thing to say.

"Long time no see…" Levi strode across the room, tan leather work boots clomping on the kitchen's ripped and stained navy linoleum floor. "How's it going?"

"Great," Travis lied, finishing up Libby's bottle by popping the nipple into the cap, then screwing on the lid before dropping the whole thing into a bowl of hot water.

"How was the rest of your day?" Levi asked Kit, pulling her in for a proprietary hug and kiss.

Travis looked away. The last thing he needed was a front-row seat to Kit and her fiancé's afternooner—especially when he fought a keen craving for one of Kit's hugs for himself.

"Mmm…" Kit said with a giggle. "It's looking up now."

Blech.

As Marlene had taught him, Travis took the bottle from the water, then squirted some onto his forearm to check the temp. Just right.

While the lovebirds kept up their cooing, Travis took Libby from her high chair, then headed for the living room rocker.

"Sorry you had to see that," he said to the munchkin in his arms once he'd settled into the comfortable wood chair.

Libby's big brown eyes widened as she suckled, her tiny fingers tightly gripping the bottle.

"I know," he teased, tickling the underside of her chin. "If you weren't so hungry, seeing them kissing would be enough to ruin your appetite, huh?"

She giggled, and a stream of formula trickled out of the corner of her mouth and down her cheek. Travis mucked it up with his tie.

"Looks like you've got Libby thoroughly charmed." Kit wandered into the room, taking a seat on a lumpy floral sofa opposite the rocker. The left sofa arm looked as if a bite had been taken out of it. White stuffing escaped the hole.

Travis shrugged. "Where's your sidekick?"

"Levi? He's out back feeding the dogs. They usually stay in the house, but when she's left alone, Cocoa gets cranky—hence the hole in the sofa." She grinned, pointing to the chewed spot Travis had already noticed. "All three dogs have been in the shed since…" Her smile faded. "Anyway, now that you'll be staying here, I imagine the pampered mutts will be glad to get back inside—although I can't say it's much cooler in here than it is in the shed. We should open some windows."

"No need," Travis said. "I was thinking of packing up Libs here and getting a motel room."

"Why?"

"Why?" He laughed. "Look at this place. "It's hardly the Taj Mahal. And if I don't get some relief from this heat, I'm liable to—"

"Figuring you wouldn't be used to our weather," Levi said, perching on the sofa arm beside Kit, "I brought a couple window units from the store. Marlene and Gary already put one in Libby's room and the master, but once we get others in the living room and kitchen, it should be more doable."

"Thanks," Travis said, "but a motel will be fine. I'll take the dogs to the pound on my way to a real-estate office to put this old place on the market."

"You're joking, right?" Kit held her hand to her throat. "Your sister and Gary loved this house and their dogs. And with the barn housing the daycare on the same mortgage, a large portion of the down payment was mine. Seeing how much Marlene wanted to fix up this place, I let her take the house."

Travis rolled his eyes. "No big deal. Just buy out my sister's share and we'll call it yours."

"It's not that easy," Kit said. "I couldn't possibly raise that much cash."

"Fine." Travis rose. Libby had long since fallen

asleep, so he planned on putting her down for a nap before tackling the job of hiring the army it would take to get the place ready to put on the market. However, if he turned the house over to Kit, then all he'd have to do until the judge ruled in his favor was hang out in a motel watching ESPN, holding Libby with one arm and working from his laptop with the other. "I'll give the house to you."

"G-GIVE IT TO ME?" KIT gulped. "No way. I couldn't possibly accept a gift that large."

"Why not? If Marlene loved this house as much as you say, she'd want you to have it."

"I agree," Levi said. "And, babe, I know we haven't set a wedding date yet, but if we're even thinking of starting that family you always talk about, this place would be a great place to do it."

"That's a good point," Kit said more softly than she'd intended. What Levi didn't realize was that if Travis was unable to unload the house easily, then…what? He might stay? The thought returned her to the night Marlene died. The desperation in her raspy voice.

He needs you. Save him, Kit. No matter what he says… Keep him in IdaBelle Falls long enough for him to learn there's more to life than—

More to life than what? What had her friend been trying to say? And why, of all places, was Kit supposed to keep Travis in IdaBelle Falls to find out?

Perhaps the even bigger question was did she even want him to stay?

No.

Yes.

Maybe.

None of which got her any closer to figuring out how to handle her first love's abrupt reentry into her life.

Chapter Four

After spending an hour helping Levi install three window air units, Travis parked himself back in the living room rocker and was about to take his first bite of that sandwich Kit had long since fixed him when a god-awful racket erupted from the kitchen.

The clacking of claws against linoleum preceded barking, then the nose-wrinkling stench of wet fur.

"Yep," Kit said, clapping her hands while three blurs of varying colors ran in a barking circle around the living room, then out into the entry hall, through the kitchen, back into the living room, only to start the whole process again. "I'd say they're happy to be out of the shed. Levi, hon? Do they have any canned food inside?"

"Already dishing it out, sweetie!" he sang from the kitchen.

Rubbing his forehead, Travis groaned.

Libby didn't know how fortunate she was to be tucked away upstairs taking a nap.

Planting his sandwich on a side table, Travis stood. Hands on his hips, he said, "This isn't going to work."

"What?" Kit asked.

"What do you think?" he said, eyeing the dogs, which were running slowly enough now that he could at least discern specific shapes and sizes. No way he could figure out what breed each dog was, seeing how not one of them had less than three distinct breed characteristics. The smallest, with a coat of rusty gray, looked part dachshund, part toy poodle, part Yorkie. The medium—Travis was hardly a dog expert—was probably a beagle-basset-Yorkie mix. The largest and by far oddest most closely resembled a black Lab, but the hair was shaggy like a Yorkie's and he sported a bulldog's flat nose. "They've got to go."

"Go where?" Kit asked. "This is their home. The smallest is Cocoa, then Gringo, then Priscilla."

"I thought the big one was a boy."

"Does she look like a boy?" Kit asked, kneeling beside the butt-ugly mutt, touching her cheek to the dog's.

Shaking his head, grinning, Travis said, "What she looks like is rabid. You might want to slowly step back, then run get a few shots."

"Don't listen to the mean man," she said to the dog, covering her shaggy ears. "He's cranky because of the heat."

Among other things, Travis thought, too exhausted to do much else besides stare incredulously as Gringo helped himself to the bologna sandwich.

"Oops," Kit said, back to giggling. "I'm sure he didn't mean to eat it. No doubt it was a reflex thing."

"No doubt," Travis said, marching into the kitchen to fix a duplicate.

Kit followed. "I'm sure in a week or so you'll love the dogs as much as Marlene and Gary did."

"Yeah," Levi said, deep-sixing three large cans of Alpo into the under-sink trash. "Gary always had a soft spot for strays. Used to tease Marlene about being his best find."

Travis choked on his first mustard-soaked bite. "He compared my sister to a stray dog?"

"Lighten up," Kit said, slipping her arm around Levi's waist. "It was a joke. Used to make Marlene howl."

Levi kissed the top of Kit's head.

Travis looked sharply away.

Along with the dogs, the lovebirds needed to go. On top of his sister's death, he was in no way ready to deal with feelings for Kit he'd thought long gone.

"What're you doing for supper?" Kit asked. "If you want, Levi and I could get you some takeout."

"Thanks," Travis said, "but I'm good. I might hit town later for a few essentials, though. Speaking of which, do you know where Marlene might've left the keys to her car?"

"Here," Kit said, walking the short distance to a wall-mounted key rack currently holding more leashes and reusable plastic bags than keys. "It's not fancy but gets the job done."

Travis rubbed his forehead.

In light of the surprises he'd already encountered, he didn't even want to imagine what his sister had found to be an acceptable ride.

"Now," Kit said, taking Levi's hand, leading him to the back door, "mothers start arriving at the daycare by five-thirty, so I'll need you to be up and alert by then. Candy Craig's usually the first one here, but she's having car trouble and her ride can't get her here till six. The two of you will have three children—and Libby—until seven-thirty, and I'll be in to help around eight-thirty, so you should be fine until—"

"Whoa," Travis said, shaking his head. "I don't do children—as in multiple kids. Libby's about all I can handle along with my regular workload."

"Sorry," she said with her usual grin, not looking remotely apologetic, "but until I find a replacement for Marlene, I was hoping you'd pitch in at the daycare. I meant to broach the subject earlier, you know, how it might be fun and educational for you to get practice with kids, but the dogs got in the way. My role these days is mainly managerial, stretching myself between all six franchises, but I'll spend as much time as I can helping you learn the ropes. From Libby you already know baby basics, and Marlene told me you're up to date on CPR through your company's course. Trust me, for the short time you're on your own, you'll do fine."

Travis growled.

"Oh, come," she said. "It'll be fun. Please?"

Lord help him, but in his already weakened emotional condition, Travis was unable to resist her charm. "I'll only be alone thirty minutes?"

"Tops." She shot him a toothy grin. Coincidentally the same one she used to wield when flirting him out of the last few M&M's back when they'd been an item.

Knowing full well he wanted his sleep as much as he'd wanted that candy, he must have been temporarily insane to blurt, "Give me a little more instruction and I'll do it."

FRIDAY AT 4:48 a.m., Travis tried putting a pillow over his head to block what felt like the third eight-point-oh earthquake of the morning. Why had he agreed to work at the daycare for even thirty minutes? And while he was asking questions, why hadn't Marlene mentioned her house being five feet from a railroad track?

Gee, probably because she knew he'd have told her to nix the deal—which, Marlene being Marlene, upon hearing his objections, would've only made her that much more determined to go through with a real-estate transaction only a train buff or a masochist would love.

Knowing he had to be up soon anyway, he grabbed his cell phone from the nightstand, putting in a call to this right-hand man to explain that his trip would take longer than expected. With a grunt he rolled out of the surprisingly comfortable black wrought-iron canopy bed. Though a little lacy for his taste, Travis would've given Gary a high five for allowing his sister to have her girlie way with the majority of the room that'd been finished in a sumptuous blend of old and new.

Antique dressers and side tables held both modern and vintage picture frames. The majority of smiling shots were of Marlene and Gary hamming it up. Newer ones included Libby. Quite a few were dog shots. Cocoa wearing a pumpkin suit for Halloween. Gringo begging. All three lounging on the front porch, tongues lolling on a sunny day.

Dark walnut floors covered in Oriental carpets laid at crazy angles shouldn't have made sense but did. The walls were covered in four varied patterns—stripes and florals and dots and checks—of pale green paper, but even this somehow worked in the atticlike room with its five dormer windows and angled ceilings.

In the bathroom, decked out in more dark walnut with an antique white porcelain claw-foot tub, it looked as if Gary had had his way with the high-tech stand-alone shower with its assortment of buttons and nozzles.

Under streaming spray Travis braced his hands against the green-brown-and-black mosaic wall, letting the water ease kinks in his neck. Being early to work was no problem, but in his office he was king. He knew what to expect.

At his sister's daycare he didn't have a clue what— or even who—might crop up. Yesterday afternoon, while Kit had still been there, he'd asked her about the kids he'd be watching, but she'd been so animated in her descriptions that all he'd focused on was her. Her and the painful memory of how and why he'd ever let what they'd shared slip away. It wasn't a topic he cared to dwell upon, leading him to rush her and Levi on their way so he could get those mangy mutts back out in the shed and himself into comfortable clothes—meaning boxers and nothing else.

The only way he'd gotten the apparently spoiled dogs outside was by flinging bologna onto the back porch as bait, then shooing them outside and shutting the door. Technically he wasn't sure whether they'd made it to the shed or not. But they were dogs. What was the worst that could happen if they spent a summer night outside?

His mind's eye flashed on those dog pics.

Then guilt settled in. The night was over now. No sense in rushing downstairs to let them in. But assuming they didn't chew anything, maybe they could come inside on probationary terms.

Travis reluctantly finished lathering and rinsing, then dressed in navy slacks, starched white shirt and red tie. In deference to his casual setting, he skipped the suit jacket. Always one step ahead of him, his receptionist had phoned his housekeeper and asked her to pack Travis a week's clothing, then meet him at the airport.

Libby had woken only once during the night, and after a quick feeding and diaper change she'd fallen right off to sleep.

In her nursery he flicked on the crystal lamp topping the dresser, then crept to her ultragirlie crib. She looked so content amongst the fuzzy pink blanket and pink gingham sheets and crib bumper that he hated waking her. He'd been surprised to see the bumper and blanket, as they'd been gifts from him. Picked from a catalogue and shipped with a brief note, maybe they hadn't held as much sentimental value as, say, a gift Marlene had received at her shower, but he was glad all the same that she'd at least liked them enough to have put them to use.

"Hey, sleepyhead," he crooned, scooping up his niece only to tuck her against his chest. How come he didn't smell this great in the morning? The scent of her pink lotion and the no-tears shampoo he'd used for her bath the previous night was still strong.

She gurgled, then fell right back asleep against him.

For a split second, unsure what to do, he vacillated between calling his secretary or, even better, Kit. But in the end he knew he'd have to start figuring out how to be a parent sooner rather than later. Besides, what if he'd called the emergency number Kit had left and Levi answered? The guy was nice and all. But Kit was one of those women who was hot but in a squeaky-clean, Mother Goose sort of way. Travis didn't much approve of her being in bed with any man—let alone a hardware store owner. Even if the guy was her fiancé.

Okay, then, he thought, gingerly heading down the stairs. Who would he approve of Kit being in bed with?

Offhand, no one.

He didn't have a clue why, but part of him felt proprietary where she was concerned, as if he'd had dibs on her under that mulberry tree all those years ago, and again at the swimming hole and even on her own bed the time her folks had gone to Little Rock for their anniversary weekend. Bottom line, if he couldn't have her, then no one else should.

Ridiculous, but there you have it. As if any of the rest of his current life made the slightest sense.

In the kitchen he switched on the light, then eyed his sleeping charge. What was the protocol on morning feedings? Did he wake Libby to feed her? Or once he scoped out the daycare, would he find a spare crib for her to crash in? Even if there was a crib, would there be a blanket?—an appropriately soft and fuzzy one?

Shaking his head, he tromped back up the stairs for the pink one from Libby's crib, then tucked it around her chubby bare legs and arms.

Back downstairs, it occurred to him that sometime during the day she'd probably need a diaper change. And what if it got cold? Sure it was June, but you never knew.

Back upstairs, he shoved a few diapers and the wipes in an oversize pink canvas tote dotted with dancing hippos. In case of sudden frost, he grabbed a mini coat and sweater from the cedar-lined closet. From the dresser he snagged three pairs of white socks. All of his finds in the bag, he repositioned Libby to his left shoulder, slung the bag over his right, then took off again for the kitchen.

Okay, back to the food issue. Now or later?

Taking a peek at Libby under the blanket—save for a small airhole, he'd put it over her head, since all those blowing air conditioners had made the house chilly—he didn't think she looked all that hungry, so he just grabbed a few bologna slices for himself.

After adding three cans of formula, a can opener and a handful of bottle liners to the diaper bag, he was almost out the door when he figured the actual bottles might also be a good idea.

He took the key ring labeled *Barn* from the rack, then aimed for the door, when the phone rang.

He jumped, as did Libby, who then started to cry.

"Crap," he said, picking up the phone. "Yes?"

"I take it you're not a morning person?" Kit asked, her chipper tone a disgustingly happy cross between sunshine and daffodils.

"Sure I am," he said, jiggling a still-whimpering Libby back to sleep. "After a gallon of coffee and a six-mile jog."

"Six miles?" she whistled. "Impressive."

Why did he get the feeling she was mocking him? "There a reason you called?"

"Just wanted to make sure you're up. And to apologize for you having to work the early shift. Or, for that matter, having to work at all. I promise to find you a replacement ASAP."

"It's not a problem," he said. "If I can handle million-dollar mergers, I can handle a few little kids."

WAAAAAAAAAAA!
"I want Mooooom-meeeeee!"
Waaaahuh! Waaaahuh!
"That's not the way you do it," said eight-year-old Lincoln Groves, who would, with any luck, march his know-it-all behind onto the IdaBelle Falls day-camp bus at seven-fifteen. As for Candy Craig, she'd called at six-ten to say she wouldn't be in at all. Travis had then phoned Kit, but she was at a center in the next county.

"Okay, then," Travis bellowed above the racket caused by two howling babies and a freaked-out pre-schooler. Pausing before slashing the entire top from the packet of toaster-strudel icing, he asked, "How about telling me the right way to open this before your little sister blows her last gasket?"

The freckle-faced kid with Batman glasses took the blunt-nosed scissors and the icing, calmly clipping the corner off the package before returning it to Travis. "Now you can draw her stupid hearts and flowers. Otherwise it would've gushed out in a big globbery pile." Shoving his glasses up his nose, he added, "She won't eat it if it doesn't have hearts and flowers."

Eyeing the packet, then the kid, Travis figured Lincoln had a point on the smaller hole making for a more efficient drawing tool. Hmph. Learn something new every day. "Thanks."

"Uh-huh." Lincoln patted his little sis on her back.

A few seconds later Travis had drawn some semblance of a heart and a flower on Clara's pastry, then plopped it on a paper plate and handed it to her.

For an all too brief instant she looked down at it, then up at him, then started screaming all over again. "This isn't right! I want Mooooooom-meeeeeee!"

Apparently Clara's show was so impressive even Libby and her pal, four-month-old Mike, stopped screeching from their high chairs long enough to look.

Sighing, Travis asked his assistant, "What now?"

"She has to sit there before she can eat. Rule number eight." He pointed toward a pint-size booth, then at a large colorful sign mounted alongside a white marker board. Sure enough, right after No Biting, was rule number eight—Always Eat at a Table. For those who couldn't yet read, pictograms got the points across.

Travis took the plate from Clara, then guided her to the booth. She calmly sat. Then, once he'd landed the pastry in front of her, she gave him a glare before digging in.

"You haven't been doing this long, have you?" Lincoln inquired.

"No. Today's my first day. But I'm getting better, don't you think?"

After fixing himself a bowl of Cheerios, Lincoln perched alongside his sister and quietly munched.

All of a sudden, the big red barn with its cow-chicken-horse-and-pig-themed wallpaper and bright white-and-red interior grew suspiciously silent.

"Everything okay?" Travis asked Clara, who'd frozen with the pastry hanging from her mouth. "Are you choking?" In case the word was too big for the little girl, he held his hands to his throat and made gagging noises.

She shook her head.

Mike and Libby giggled.

"You're funny," Lincoln said.

"Thanks," Travis said, shoulders proudly straightening. This was a tough crowd. "Any idea what's bugging your sister?"

Frowning, the boy nodded.

"Well?" Travis asked, wrinkling his noise at the sudden foul smell. Had Libby or Mike dropped a bomb in their diapers?

Clara started wailing again, and apparently not wanting to be left out, Libby and Mike joined in.

"What's the matter?" Travis shouted above the racket to the little girl.

"She prob'ly pooped in her pants," Lincoln said. "She always gets that look and cries when she does 'cause she can't chew and poop at the same time. Plus, she's s'posed to be potty trained, so she thinks Mom's gonna be mad."

Sure. Made perfect sense. If you were nearly three.

"Clara, sweetie," Travis said, "let's somehow get you cleaned up."

"I want *Mooooom-meeeeee!*"

"Waaaaaa huuuuh," wailed Libby.

"Argh waaaaaaaa," cried Mike.

"You're supposed to do somethin'," Lincoln oh-so-helpfully pointed out, looking bored with his hands flattened over his ears.

Ruff! Ruff! Ruff!

Travis had to look twice to make sure he wasn't hallucinating. But sure enough, as if he didn't have enough going on already, all three dogs bounded into the room.

"How did they get in here?" Travis asked, scooping Libby, then Mike, into his arms while trying to shoo the dogs back out the open rear door. "And how did the door get open?"

"Prob'ly Clara," Lincoln matter-of-factly said, not budging an inch from the snack table to actually help. "I bet she did while you were getting the cereal and milk."

"Did you do that?" Travis asked the still-bawling girl.

"Oops," Lincoln said, spilling a waterfall of red Kool-Aid off the snack table and onto the formerly pristine white tile floor.

The smallest dog lapped at the sweet puddle. The other two joined in.

"That's not sanitary," his bigmouthed assistant said.

Waaaaaa huh!

Argggggggg huhhhhh!

Ruff! Ruff!!

Racking his brain for a way to at least calm the babies, Travis double jiggled, then launched into an animated rendition of the wiener song. "Oooh, I wish I were an—"

Blech. Mike yakked all over Travis's formerly crisp white shirt. The slimy heat of a neon-orange breakfast of pureed peaches oozed down his chest.

Woof! Woof!

Hands still over his ears, Lincoln shook his head. "You're gonna get fired for being such a bad babysitter."

Just when Travis thought things couldn't possibly get worse than three screaming, barfing kids, three licking, wriggling, barking dogs and one know-it-all eight-year-old, Kit burst through the back door. Judging by the size of her frown, he was about to be fired.

But then, in light of his current situation, was getting axed really such a bad thing?

"WHAT IN THE WORLD'S going on?" Kit asked, standing at the edge of the daycare's chaos, hands on her hips. But was there really even a need to ask, seeing how the obvious answer was that in under an hour, Travis had single-handedly destroyed the once precision-run space? He'd been so surprisingly wonderful with Libby, she'd expected him to have few problems. But then he was only supposed to have been alone with the children for thirty minutes.

Toys and muddy dog prints littered the usually immaculate floor, and she didn't even want to know *what* Cocoa was concentrating so hard on licking. *Eeew,* she thought, pinching her nose while leading Gringo and Priscilla out the back door. What was that smell?

"Want me to return to the house?" Travis shouted

above the kids. "I'm thinking that around here I'm in the way."

She shot him a death-ray stare that said, in body language even Clara could understand, that he'd better not budge an inch.

After closing the two biggest dogs into the fenced portion of the yard behind the house, Kit headed back inside to find a giggling Lincoln on the floor getting his face washed by Cocoa's tongue.

Travis was still jiggling babies and singing the wiener song, but judging by the infants' high-pitched tones, they were more in the mood for rock.

"Lincoln, honey," she said, kneeling in front of the little boy.

"Uh-huh?"

"Do you remember where Miss Marlene put her dogs?"

"Uh-huh."

"Do you think you could do me a big favor and carry Cocoa outside to the backyard?"

"Yeah. I told Mr. Travis he was gonna get fired for lettin' 'em in."

"I didn't *let* them in," Travis argued. "Clara left the back door open."

"That's low," she said, scooping up the stinky toddler. "How could she possibly reach high enough to unlock it?"

"You calling me a liar?" Travis said.

Giving him another look on her way to the changing table, she pursed her lips and shook her head.

"Yep," Lincoln said, hands on his hips. "She's callin' you a liar. What're you gonna do? Quit?"

Tempting. Highly tempting. But then Libby stilled, resting her head on Travis's shoulder, nuzzling her downy hair against his neck. Mike followed suit. Suddenly, Travis was no longer incompetent but king of the world.

"Nope," Travis said, "I'm not going to quit."

He glanced up to find Kit back in the room, still scowling, but looking sexy in a preschool teacher sort of way. It was then he knew toughing out this temporary assignment wasn't just about growing more connected with his darling niece, but becoming closer to the one woman he should've never let get away.

Chapter Five

"I'm sorry," Kit said to Travis an hour later. Even though Lincoln had gotten on the day-camp bus and nine more children under the age of four had come to take his place, she and Miss Chrissy—a twenty-year-old mom wannabe/nutritionist who adored kids—had long since gotten things under control. Chrissy had come as soon as Kit had sent out an emergency call. But as Chrissy had needed a quick shower, she had still taken a while.

"'Bout what?" he asked, standing at the kitchen sink with his shirtsleeves rolled up and his hands in soapy water, washing primary-colored plastic bowls, plates and cups. His forearms were muscular and tanned; images of him on his morning jog in front of a glistening Lake Michigan flashed before her eyes. Though his poor shirt hung wrinkled and limp and covered with baby barf, and his usually neat dark hair hung at a rakish slant over his right eye, Kit had never seen him look more handsome.

"I, um…" She licked her lips, scolding herself for thinking him handsome when she had date with Levi that night. But then, what was the problem in that? Just because she was engaged didn't mean she couldn't still appreciate another man's assets. *Or remember the outrageous pleasure those assets used to bring.* Or wonder what if things had turned out differently between them. But why? Travis had hurt her. So why did she now find herself attracted to him all over again?

She cleared her throat. "I'm sorry about accusing you of leaving the door open. While climbing on the bus, Lincoln confessed. He said he wanted to get Clara in trouble because she chewed the wheel off his favorite Hot Wheels Corvette."

"Sure," Travis said. "No harm done."

"Well, I didn't want you to think I blamed you for—"

"Let's face it," he said, "I'm better in the boardroom than the playroom."

"I wouldn't say that." She landed a teasing elbow to his midsection, only to encounter the hard heat of his abs. *Whoa.* Reddening, she inched away. What was that old saying about looking, not touching? "Besides, this is only your first day. Before Libby's custody hearing goes to court you'll have plenty of time to get the hang of the babysitting biz."

"Great." After rinsing the last red plastic cup, he plucked the stopper from the sink and dried his hands on a yellow dish towel. "And here I've been hoping you'd tell me that after today I wasn't welcome back and that the leave of absence I've arranged isn't necessary."

"You wish," she said with a light pat to his shoulder, which was also rock-hard. What was wrong with her? Why couldn't she keep her hands off him? Why did she even want him there? Sure, Marlene seemed to have wanted Travis to stay in IdaBelle Falls, but that didn't mean he had to be at the daycare all that time. So why was she encouraging him to remain on staff? Honestly, she liked him, wanted to be with him. In subtle ways, he reminded her of Marlene, meaning she was, in a sense, using him for comfort, right?

That was all well and good, but shouldn't Levi be the one she turned to?

"Absolutely." He winked. "That's exactly what I'm wishing. I've never figured myself for the early-retirement type, but in this case…"

"Seriously," she said, slotting her hands in her jean pockets—just in case she got another craving to sample his goods! "It does get easier. But if you're looking for something a little more in your safety zone, the books need to be done."

"That sounds—"

"Hey," Chrissy said, ducking into the fridge for her ever-present water bottle. At four-ten, she was plump, blond and perky and on a perpetual diet. After a long swig she said, "The crew's temporarily occupied for the two seconds it takes to cut their melons." She was referring to the green-construction-paper watermelon cutouts the children were making for their art project. Brown M&M's would be the seeds, but so far more had been gobbled than pasted. "Travis, how are you liking your new job?"

"So far I've had more fun having my appendix taken out." He chuckled, but it wasn't much of a stretch to see from the sadness behind his eyes that he'd meant what he'd said. He was miserable. But did that misery stem from a tough patch with the kids or the situation in general? Was it that he was so far from his natural element? Not only was he still trying to deal with grief from Marlene's death but also coming to grips with a foreign lifestyle. In return for the comfort he'd inadvertently brought her, how might she help him?

"Mmm, we're that much fun, huh?" Chrissy said with another swig of water and a wink before jogging back to the kids.

"You okay?" Kit asked Travis once Chrissy was out of earshot.

"What do you mean?" he asked, gazing past red-and-white-plaid curtains to the overgrown yard and sad dogs and even sadder house. He rubbed the back of his neck.

"I mean…" she said, quietly stepping up behind him, squelching the urge to massage away his tension. Why, whenever she was near him, did she feel as if time had stood still and that the years dividing them had vanished? "Whatever's on your mind seems heavier than Clara's loaded diaper."

Still not facing her, he shrugged. "Guess the gravity of this—Marlene's and Gary's deaths..." He shook his head. Sighed. "Doesn't matter. Maybe the funeral tomorrow will at least help me gain closure. Show me the way to those books?"

"Yeah," she said, her throat tightening at the raw pain in his expression. She wanted to help him feel better. Per his sister's dying wish, she wanted to show him there was more to life than work. Than the weighty sense of honor and obligation to his grandfather that, according to Marlene, he'd always felt since his own dad had skipped out on the family business, cashing out his trust fund and never looking back. But how was she supposed to show Travis all that when so far all he'd done since hitting IdaBelle Falls city limits was struggle? Struggle with Beulah, Libby, the heat, the house, the dogs and now the daycare. Despite this, the part of her still carrying baggage from their nebulous breakup over a decade earlier asked why she should care if he was having a rough time? Granted, with Travis living in Chicago, they'd never had much of a future. So why had she slept with him back then? Simple—she'd loved him. And now? She no longer harbored any ill will. She'd forgiven him. Because of his loss, the challenge he faced in raising Libby, Kit, above all, felt sorry for him.

She could still be angry at him for his cowardly behavior, but why? She was happily engaged and, if anything, she'd learned from her experience with Travis. Namely that when it came to romance, she needed to keep her feet firmly on the ground. "Come on," she said, leading him to the child-safety gate at the foot of the loft stairs. "I'm sure our office isn't anywhere near as efficient as yours, but so far it seems to have gotten the job done."

"How are things?" he asked, following her up the first stair, then latching the gate behind them. "With the business?"

"Good," she said, too aware of not only him being behind her but what they'd done the last time they'd been together in a loft. Here she was supposed to be helping him work through his pain, but suddenly all she could think about was that he had a full view of her butt!

Finally at the stairs' top, she headed to the largest of the two desks placed alongside each other in front of matching paned windows that'd plugged up the old hay doors. Each desk held an older-model computer and neat stacks of papers, along with an assortment of handcrafted items ranging from clay ashtrays to papier-mâché mush-rooms to milk-carton Easter baskets still loaded with sticky jelly beans that should've long since been thrown out, but neither Kit nor Marlene had had the heart.

Unlike the portion of the barn the kids used, the loft had remained cosmetically mostly untouched. Hundred-year-old plank floors had been sanded and varnished, then covered in spots with colorful rag rugs. Cozy armchairs and floor lamps and an abundance of ferns and ivies and a ragtag assortment of other potted plants provided the perfect homey touches to unfinished-wood-paneled walls.

"Nice," Travis said, taking in the place. He didn't remember their wild time in a space much like this, did he?

"Thanks."

"Best part's that up here, I'm away from those mangy dogs."

"Oh, now, you don't mean that," she said with a laugh. "Give 'em a few days. They'll grow on you." Just like IdaBelle Falls. Travis once seemed happy here. What had happened to change that? How did she reconnect him to the boy he used be? Which was undoubtedly the task Marlene had truly wanted from her. "Which reminds me—what were the dogs doing outside the fence? If they're not in the house or the shed, they're supposed to be in the fenced portion of the yard."

"I'm thinking last night," he said, rubbing his dark-stubbled jaw, "I might've shooed them out the door. Couple times with Libby, things got tense."

"Sure, but that doesn't mean you can just kick the dogs out of their house. They live here, Travis."

"Correction," he said, standing so close she felt lost in his shadow. Had he always been this big? Powerful? Smelled like expensive aftershave and baby lotion and pureed peaches? "I live there now, and if I say the dogs go, they go. Period."

"You can't do that. Marlene loved those dogs, as

did Gary. They'd saved each of them after finding them abandoned on the side of the road."

"And...?" he said, gesturing her to move her story along. "I'm not Marlene and Gary. Quit trying to mold me into some handy dandy replacement."

"I can't believe you," she said with an angry shake of her head. "What happened? You used to be—"

"What?" he asked, stepping another inch closer, thoroughly invading what precious little remained of her personal space and muddied mind. Up close like this, she couldn't think—even breathe. Her heart didn't seem to be working right. Instead of its normal steady beat, her pulse flashed erratic and heavy. What was wrong with her? He was just a guy. So, yeah, she might've shared her first real kiss with him—not to mention her virginity—but big whoop. It wasn't as if she hadn't made love since then.

Yeah, but how many lovemaking sessions had meant as much as that first? How many lonely nights had she relived, rehashed, regretted every nuance of what they'd shared?

But she shouldn't get carried away. He'd left town once and would do it again. Which was significant why? If Travis came or went, what did she care?

"What do you perceive as being wrong with me? Lots of people don't like dogs mucking up their homes. Just because I'm not comfortable around kids doesn't mean I don't like them. On our own last night, just the two of us, Libby and I eventually got along just fine."

"Did I say you didn't?" she asked, scowling.

"You implied—"

"Did not."

"Did."

"Didn't. In fact, I—"

He stopped her midspeech with a kiss.

But this was no ordinary kiss; this one rocked her to her core. Not in its hardness or softness or even shock value. It was something far more elusive—and dangerous. Not remotely in a physical sense but an emotional one.

As he pulled away and stormed to his sister's desk, she stood there alone, dazed and touching her lips. The wonder of his kiss was in the bewildering fact that it'd acted as a key unlocking a long-hidden portion of her heart. For Travis hadn't just given her her first kiss but first love. Even as she was cognizant of the fact that she needed to get back downstairs, to the children and her normal life, her feet felt cemented to the loft's smooth wood planks.

Staring at the broad planes of Travis's back, she wanted to ease her hands over them, kneading away knots. Most of all she wanted to see him smile, not just help him come to grips with the present situation but be the one responsible for returning light to his eyes.

All of which was crazy.

Which was why she said, "Guess you know how to run a computer, so help yourself. If you need anything…I'll be downstairs. Oh, and if you ever kiss me again…" What? What would she toss out as her big threat? Though she'd never admit it, at the moment the only shameful thing she could say with any grain of truth was that if he tried kissing her again, she might just kiss him back.

She'd reached the first step down when he called out, "Wait. Kit, please—wait."

Though her mind told her to run, she froze.

"I—I'm sorry," he said. "What I just did—the kiss…" She turned in time to see him shake his head. "It was bullheaded and inappropriate and I'm sorry. It won't happen again."

"Th-thanks for that," she said, words clipped and formal. "The apology. And please do…see that it doesn't happen again."

She wanted to marry Levi without wondering "what if" or having any regrets. The last thing she needed was a refresher course in Travis's expert kissing, making her wonder if she'd made the right choice.

"YOU OKAY?"

From what Travis had thought was a secluded tree, well away from the few mourners lingering alongside Marlene's and Gary's graves, he looked up to see Kit strolling his way. Great. Just what he needed. As if this moment couldn't get worse, now he had to share his intensely private grief. "I'm fine," he said from between gritted teeth, willing himself not to break down here. Not just yet. "We're fine."

"Want me to take her?" she asked, cupping her hand to Libby's downy hair.

"No," he said, gripping the infant closer.

"It was a lovely service," Kit murmured.

He laughed. "Why is that the first thing anyone says at a funeral? Seriously, think about it. What's remotely *lovely* about putting two young, vibrant—dead—people in the ground?"

"I didn't mean it like that," she said. "And for the record, I'm hurting every bit as much as you." As if proving her point, she removed her oversize black sunglasses, revealing swollen, bloodshot eyes that looked as if she'd been crying all night.

"Sorry," he said reflexively.

She shrugged. "I see you're still doing it?"

"What?"

"Swallowing your feelings. Forcing yourself to be strong."

"You don't even know me," he said. "What the hell business is it of yours what I feel?"

Now she laughed past a sniffle and fresh tears. After glancing over her shoulder, she said in a low tone, "I don't know you? We spent an entire summer together, Travis."

"That was a million years ago."

"Not to me."

"What's that supposed to mean?" Since he didn't want her answer any more than he currently wanted her company, he kissed the crown of Libby's head, then took off across the grassy knoll, sidestepping headstones, absorbing a hundred years of other families' grief.

"I mean," she said, doggedly on his heels, "that for me, anyway, that summer feels like yesterday. And it's not that big a stretch to remember that, even back then you had this knack for walling yourself off. Remember when Marlene fell from Vince Master's tree house? And she screamed bloody murder the whole time we were in the car with Vince's mom? The rest of us were scared out of our minds, but not you. You just kept a tight hold of her hand, telling her to calm down, everything would be fine. Like this teen grown-up, you had her insurance card in your wallet. Do you know how bizarre we all thought that was?" Out of breath, she tugged on his arm, dragging him to a stop alongside a massive white marble monument to Felix Goodwilly, one of the town's first mayors. Dappled shade somewhat cooled the sweltering midday sun. "It wasn't so much that you were prepared to handle any emergency but that everything did turn out all right. She only had a sprained ankle and a minor concussion. It was as if you possessed the sheer will to bend fate in your favor."

"If that's so," he said lightly rocking Libby, "I'm doing a helluva job right about now."

"Oh, my God, would you listen to yourself? As if there was anything you could've done to right this horrible wrong."

"But I want to," he whispered, his voice raw.

"What?"

"Fix this. I want Marlie back," he said, squeezing his sister's baby, remembering all the times he'd held

Marlene, playing surrogate parent when either their parents had been too busy or their paternal grandparents too tired. Like a slide show in his head, he saw his sister at four, hiding in a gloomy interior corner of the imposing stone church the family attended because some kid told her the gargoyles guarding the pulpit would eat her for Sunday dinner. He saw her again in third grade, when she'd accidentally superglued her fingers together and had been afraid they'd always be stuck that way. Again in middle school, when she'd bombed her first algebra test and was sure she wouldn't get into a good college. All those times, he'd held her, told her not to be frightened. That everything would be better. And in turn, even though she'd been younger than he, there'd been plenty of times she'd returned the favor. Telling him it would be okay when a girlfriend had broken up with him or when he'd tossed a football into one of his grandmother's prized sculptures.

Seeing all that, reliving it heartbeat for heartbeat in his mind, snapped something deep inside him. With Marlene gone, who was left to tell him everything would be okay? Who was left to fight battles for? Who would—

He choked back a strangled sob, willing himself not to cry, but as if in losing his sister, he'd lost the will to maintain always impeccable composure, tears fell and showed no signs of stopping.

Kit reached out to him. And at first, not wanting to share this intensely private, painful moment, he turned his back to her, pouring out his love and frustration and loss into Libby. But Kit refused him his space, stepping up behind him, enfolding both him and his sister's beautiful child.

In an impossibly sweet voice she said, "Everything is going to be all right, you know?"

He shook his head. "No. Never again. Beulah's going to somehow win custody of Libby. And who am I to say she shouldn't? I don't know the first thing about raising a family, seeing how—"

"Stop," Kit said, turning him to face her. "That's a load of bull. According to Marlene, you were all the family she needed rolled into one."

"Then why did she leave Chicago?"

"For her own sanity. That's why she wanted you to leave, as well. Because she saw the futility in you trying to single-handedly maintain a billion-dollar empire. Oh, sure, you have every task delegated down to the last mop and I don't know—" she fought for a grin "—computer chip. But at the end of the day, Marlene thought you carried the weight of the world squarely on your shoulders. She didn't want that for herself, but most especially she didn't want it for the brother she'd loved so dearly."

Her touch at first tentative, Kit raised her fingers to the furrow between Travis's eyes. He flinched, but then the tears were back—or maybe they'd never left—and she was cupping his cheek and he was leaning into her touch.

"That's right," she crooned, "let it go. No one can be one hundred percent *on* all the time, Travis. Not even almighty you."

THAT NIGHT, LYING ON THE lumpy sofa in his sister's dark living room, thirty minutes after putting Libby to bed, blustery air-conditioning blowing on his bare chest and legs, Travis finally dared exhale. Finally allowed himself not just to listen to Kit's words, but truly hear.

A week earlier, if someone had told him he'd be in this position, he'd have called them a fool to their face. Less than forty-eight hours earlier, he'd been in control of everything. Had the world by the balls. At the moment, the only thing eluding him was that whole tricky issue of life and death. Even though he'd thought he had everything under control, he hadn't been able to save Marlene or Gary. Hell, he hadn't even known they were gone. As much as he loved his sister, you'd have thought the moment her soul left Earth he'd have, at the very least, sensed a disruption in his life.

And so what did that ultimately say about him? The fact that it'd been Kit telling him they were gone. Did he truly have control over anything? Or was it all just a big illusion? A game in which he was someone's pawn?

That endless summer in IdaBelle Falls, he'd felt a powerful sense of belonging. Like his sister, he'd never wanted to leave. But then he'd gotten back to the real world and realized all good things must come to an end. Yes, for the first time ever in this small town he'd felt part of something special, but therein lay the kicker. That feeling? It'd been temporary. Intangible. There only for that all-too-brief summer. Even at seventeen he'd known he had future responsibilities that couldn't be put aside for some sappy emotion like love—if that had even been what he'd felt for Kit. But if it hadn't been love, why had giving her up hurt so bad? Why had his fingertips itched to dial her number so long after? Why, to this day, did he feel so guilty for not having the courage to at least make a clean break?

And why now, when he should've been catching up on the latest merger news, was he in such a spiraling downward funk?

From across the room, on the hacked-off section of shag carpet in front of the brick mantel, the littlest dog looked up and whined. Cocked her head—that much he remembered about her, that she was a she. The big dogs kept on with their naps.

Travis never would've let them inside but the day had been powerful hot. And something Kit had said the previous afternoon—no, the way she'd looked at him after asking what was wrong with him, as if she was disappointed with what he'd become—had ticked him off. Made him more determined than ever to prove he could achieve as big a victory with his current responsibilities as he had with Rose Industries.

"I'm a wild success," he said to the goofy little dog. "Everyone thinks so."

The mutt just kept staring.

"The only reason I let you in wasn't because of anything Kit said but out of love for my sister."

The dog stood, stretched, then leisurely strolled to park herself under his hand, which he'd draped off the sofa.

"Be careful," he said, giving the soft spots behind her curly-haired ears a rub. "According to Kit, I'm not worthy of your attention."

The dog obviously must not have cared since she hung around for more.

Why did he care—about what Kit thought, that is? And why had he kissed her? What had he been thinking? More to the point, why *hadn't* he been thinking? Obviously a temporary-insanity kind of thing, as the kiss hadn't meant anything. He'd just seen her standing there, drenched in sunlight, and for an instant he'd been seventeen again. And happy— if only for a brief while.

The phone rang, and this time, instead of the dog moaning, it was Travis, because the closest phone was all the way in the kitchen.

Grunting, Travis pushed up from the sofa and wound his way into the equally dark kitchen, lit only by the wash of moonlight eking past open curtains. He would've just let the phone ring, but seeing how his cell had gone missing—he halfway suspected either Lincoln or Clara ate it—he figured the caller might be someone from his office trying to track him down.

"Hello?" he said on the seventh ring.

"Hey." The soft, wholly feminine voice belonged to Kit. His chest tightened, fingers clenching around the old-fashioned handset.

"Yes?" he asked, resenting the hold she apparently still had on him after all these years.

"I just wanted to…"

"I'm listening," he said, perching on the edge of a step stool. Cocoa had wandered into the kitchen and now used his right dark-sock-clad foot for a pillow.

"I don't know why I called," she said. "I just—I felt sad about the way we left things."

"Me, too," he said, kneeling to pick up the dog, hugging it close. The warm fur felt nice against his bare chest. Comforting, like a heated fuzzy blanket. Crazy. Calming, the way Kit's hugs had been healing at the cemetery. The ultimate tranquilizers—until Levi wandered up, suggesting they get a move on so as not to be late to the wake.

"For the record," he said, "again, I'm sorry about…you know. The kiss." The equally crazy—albeit wonderful—kiss that'd been so out of character for him he might as well have been having an out-of-body experience. It was nuts, but what was he supposed to do about it? It was a little late for takebacks now.

"Yes," she said, her voice a raspy—and yes, sexy—whisper. "I know. But that isn't why I called."

"Oh?"

"Travis… Guess it's my turn to apologize if I'm overstepping here, but Marlene, on her deathbed, asked something of me, and at the time I chalked up her request to pain meds."

"And…?" He squeezed the little dog tighter, and as if it were a baby every bit as much as Libby, Cocoa fell asleep with her head on Travis's shoulder. He closed his eyes, no longer fighting tears for his lost sister, for the lost promise of her life. He didn't want to cry for her, but he silently did. Openly mourning felt like an admission of her death, and he wasn't ready for that. Not anywhere near ready. Granted he'd had a meltdown at the cemetery, but part of him still thought that any second she and Gary would burst through the back door, shouting *Surprise!* He'd find that all of this had just been some whacked game designed by Marlene to get him out of the office and into her small town way of life she'd been forever trying to convince him might've been a viable option for his own life's journey.

"I keep asking you if you're okay," Kit said, jolting him from his grief to the present. "And you keep assuring me you are, but—"

"You're right," he haltingly, begrudgingly said. "I'm not well."

"Are you sick?" she asked, alarm in her voice.

"No," he said, stroking the dog's right ear. "At least not the way you think. Guess I'm just having a tough time coming to grips with…"

"Don't rush it," she urged. "Losing your sister has to be quite a shock. It's only been a few days, Travis. You can't expect yourself to—"

"I know." It'd been on the tip of his tongue to fight. To tell her he had responsibilities he couldn't just up and abandon. But a funny thing had happened at the funeral that afternoon. It'd dawned on him that he was fallible. He was human. Life was short. Rose Industries was a well-oiled machine that, last time he'd checked, was chugging along fine without him. "I know I should take time to grieve, but that doesn't mean I can hide here forever, wiping noses and making bottles and—"

"Two days, Travis," she'd softened her voice, and in the dark kitchen, even over the static-filled phone, her velvety tone stroked him like a caress. "Give yourself room to heal. Let me help."

How deeply attractive that sounded. Returning to her for more of her special brand of comfort. But was it smart? The woman was engaged. Yes, he might've had an epiphany regarding his lot in life, but that didn't mean he was about to throw in the towel on his career and hang out on street corners, singing folk songs.

"I've got to go," he lied. "Libby's crying."

"O-okay," she said. "I didn't mean to interrupt your evening. I just—"

"Thanks, Kit, but I've really got to go."

Before she said anything to stop him, he hung up the phone. Before he grew one heartbeat more attached. What they'd shared had been amazing, but they'd been kids. Now, he suspected he was using her as a sort of instant replacement for his sister. Kit had been Marlene's best friend. They were similar in so many ways. It was only natural he'd be attracted to her—as a friend, right?

To keep whatever he felt for her in check, he needed to put on a happy face and prove not just to her but to the world that he had a complete handle on this entire situation. Even if inside he feared he might be falling apart.

KIT HUNG UP THE KITCHEN phone and stared out at her overgrown backyard, awash in moonlight. How many happy times she and Levi and Marlene and Gary had spent on the patio. Laughing over homemade sangria and nachos. They'd planned future vacations and new avenues to explore with the daycares. What they hadn't planned on was half their group not making it to their thirtieth birthdays.

Arms crossed, letting tears slowly fall, Kit ached not only for herself but for Travis. And Libby. Poor, poor Libby.

As the child's godmother, Kit, too, had a stake in the girl's life. At a simple private christening ceremony Travis hadn't been able to attend, Kit had sworn to protect and watch over the infant. Travis had done the same, making them an oddly matched team. Did that explain her all-consuming compulsion as of late to be with him? Talk to him? Touch him?

Marlene had been good friends with Levi, but it hadn't been a secret she'd really wanted her brother and Kit to end up together. When it'd appeared that was about as likely as IdaBelle Falls hosting the

Olympics, Marlene had given up. At least Kit had thought she had.

Stinging eyes closed, Kit journeyed back to the night of her best friend's death... .

"Come closer..."

Kit had abided by Marlene's wish, inching closer to the emergency room bed, trying so hard to look past the severely bruised right side of Marlene's pretty face. The left had been bandaged to such a degree Kit had feared what was beneath the garishly white gauze, but not as much as she'd feared her friend's prognosis.

Only an hour earlier Marlene and her husband of three years had been out for a much-anticipated night of two-stepping. Ever since giving birth to Libby, Marlene had been so wrapped up in being a great mom she'd seemingly all but forgotten how much fun she used to have being a great dancer and wife.

For Marlene, that night was supposed to have been about reconnecting with the fun and still vibrantly sexy woman inside—not about losing her best friend and soul mate, Gary. Certainly not about then losing her own life to something as senseless as fog and a too-tired semi driver cutting a curve too close on an unseasonably cool Saturday night.

"Don't you give up," Kit had said. Though tears had flowed freely, she'd made no attempt to hide them or wipe them away. "You have so much to live for... Gary might be gone, but little Libby. Don't you leave her..."

"She's yours now," Marlene had said, her raspy voice barely rising above the erratic beeps and hums of the machines keeping her alive. "You and Travis. Together..."

"No," Kit had said with a sniffle and a vehement shake of her head, somehow finding air past the cloying scents of iodine and antiseptic. "Libby needs you—her mom."

"I always thought you'd make a beautiful couple. J-just like Gary and me." She'd paused for a faint smile.

"Don't you die," Kit had implored, gripping her friend's hand tighter, as if pleading could keep her alive.

"Together...you and Travis raise Libby. He needs you. Save him, Kit. No matter what he says. Keep him in IdaBelle Falls long enough for him to learn there's more to life than—" Her words had melded into a fit of harsh coughs.

"Libby needs *you*," Kit had repeated, barely able to see her friend through messy tears. "*I* do. The kids at the daycares. You mean so much to so many people." With her free hand Kit had gingerly cupped her best friend's cheek, trying not to notice how the whites of her eyes were blood-streaked or that her pupils weren't focused in the same direction. The beep indicating Marlene's pulse had sped up, then slowed, slowed until Kit's own breathing mirrored the beep that was now down to one every three or four seconds. Throat tight, stomach sick, Kit had swiped more tears with the back of her free hand. "Don't you die on me. Don't..."

Too late. Her best friend was already gone.

Chapter Six

"You're really bad at this," Lincoln said to Travis bright and early Monday morning while Travis struggled to unstick and then refasten Libby's diaper tape.

"Thanks," Travis said, pulling the legs down on her yellow jumper, being careful to properly fasten the snaps, as opposed to getting them crooked as he'd done the previous morning.

What he wouldn't give to pay someone to handle the whole diaper issue while he went for a run. But then, wasn't that how his parents had raised him? Hiring people to perform his and his sister's basic care. He hadn't liked it. So how could he turn around and do the same thing to his niece? He couldn't—wouldn't. Making him doubly determined to accomplish all things associated with her care.

Over the weekend, in between pop-in visits from Beulah he suspected were more in the range of inspections than social visits, then catching up on company paperwork, e-mails and calls to his key people, Travis had thought he'd gotten much more proficient at all things baby. Apparently Lincoln didn't agree.

The boy said, "Clara swallowed my favorite Mustang last night."

"Her mouth's big enough," Travis said with a grin, swooping a cooing Libby into the air, then tucking her against his chest. "But somehow that sounds a little far-fetched." Regardless of whether they were talking a car or a horse!

Scrunching his nose, the boy asked, "What's that mean?"

"That I think you just told me a whopper." Travis ruffled the kid's hair. What made the story even more unconvincing was that Clara was looking perfectly healthy at the snack table, munching dry Froot Loops with her chubby fingers. "Kind of like the other day when you told me she was the one who'd opened the door to let the dogs in, right?"

The boy looked to his feet.

"Do you and Clara not get along?" Travis asked, settling Libby into her high chair alongside Mike.

"I dunno. I just don't like her very much. Mommy loves her more."

"Oh, now, I don't believe that for a second." He gave both babies graham crackers to maul, then popped a toaster strudel in the toaster for Lincoln.

"It's true. She gets tucked in first, and in the morning she gets to sleep later. Last night she dropped her pie all over the floor and Mommy gave her a second piece. I'd've made her clean it up and go to bed."

"Ms. Marlene was my little sister," Travis said while waiting for the toaster to do its thing.

"I miss her, but she's in Heaven," the boy said matter-of-factly.

Travis wished he could be as frank. But then again, wouldn't that be admitting Marlene was really and truly gone? Which, of course, she was. But would it be so bad to pretend she was around just a few more days? Maybe because of all those times they'd been forced to attend prim-and-proper services in starched finery, as an adult Travis wasn't all that keen on church. Hell, after what'd happened to Marlene and Gary, was he even all that big of a believer in God? One thing he was sure of: assuming there was a better place after death, Marlene and her husband would be there.

"Good morning," Kit said, sailing through the barn's back door. "Have a nice weekend?"

"Morning," Travis said, the verdict still out on whether the weekend had been good or not. More than anything, it'd been weird. He'd been on his own his whole life, but in posh palaces with housekeepers and cooks.

"Sorry to have left you high and dry. I was a bridesmaid in a friend's wedding in Fayetteville. I love weddings, and this one was amazing and provided a much-needed change of mood. Anyway—sorry to abandon you."

"It's okay," he said, inordinately pleased that she'd been out of town and therefore hadn't purposely avoided him. "I did have a couple visits from Beulah."

"Really?" She removed a light denim jacket, hanging it over her purse on a wall hook. "How was that?"

He shrugged. "Better than a root canal."

"That good, huh?" She grinned.

Clara leaped from the snack table to hug Kit; Lincoln followed.

"I'm impressed," Kit said after hugging both kids. "Looks like you've got everything under control." Candy Craig had quit the previous week, leaving him temporarily on his own for the morning shift, which, surprisingly enough, he was starting to enjoy.

Travis shrugged, then yawned.

"Libby keep you up?"

"Trains."

She made a sympathetic clucking sound. "You'll get used to them. At least that's what Marlene said."

"Hope she was right." He shoved his hands in his pockets. "Anyway, I couldn't sleep, so I dived into the books. You aware of how far into the red the business is?"

She crossed to the babies to softly stroke their heads. "All businesses operate at a loss for the first few years, don't they?"

"If the owners like throwing away money."

"We're doing the best we can," she said. "There are only so many—"

"Skip the excuses." Withdrawing a spreadsheet from his shirt pocket, he unfolded it, then pointed at the many red areas. "I broke it down and two are running way under capacity. Even with the relatively small population base of the area, with the right advertising you could double attendance."

"But advertising's expensive."

"So is operating at a loss."

She got a freshly laundered wash rag from a basketful on the counter, wet it, then began washing cheeks. "If we had more children, that would mean hiring more staff."

"And? What's the problem with that?"

"If we don't have cash for advertising, we sure don't have—"

"Ever heard the saying 'You have to spend money to make it'?" Standing behind her, he accidentally caught a whiff of her hair. Honeysuckle. For a split second he closed his eyes and was instantly transported to their summer.

Honeysuckle vines surrounded his grandmother's home, and each time Kit had bounded up the porch steps in her flip-flops, he'd stepped out the screen door, trying to be cool and unaffected about the way sun glinted off the red streaks in her dark hair. Or how his fingertips itched from wanting to skim along her collarbone and bare shoulders when she wore her pink tube top.

She spun to face him and he had to learn to breathe all over again. Maybe it was the sleek column of her throat or her full lips or those eyes that always seemed to want more from him—expect more—that had him feeling like a gawky teen instead of the CEO he was. Or maybe it was Marlene's death that had him all screwed up inside, wanting to reclaim the one thing he'd sometimes felt he'd searched his whole life to find but had always been just beyond his reach. A real family that ate together and played together and acted as a unit as opposed to virtual strangers living under the same roof. His grandparents had loved him and Marlene, they just hadn't been the best at showing it. Hell, maybe they hadn't even known how. Here, in IdaBelle Falls, for that brief, shining time, he'd felt a part of something bigger than himself—or even his grandparents' complex goals that kept him on a driven course. Trouble was, Kit was just Kit. She wasn't family—hell, she was barely even his friend. His last remaining family member was Libby, and she couldn't even talk. So where did that leave him?

Hands on her hips, chin raised, his new business partner said, "Ever heard the saying 'You have to have money to spend it'?"

"Okay, look," he said, willing to do anything to get his mind back on work instead of stealing another taste of her lips. "How about if I take care of the advertising?"

"But I already told you we—"

"It'll be my gift."

"But Marlene didn't want you paying for—"

"Consider it a loan. I'll track everything I spend, and then when we're firmly in the black, you can repay me. Deal?" He stuck out his hand for her to shake, and when she molded her fingers to his, he fought the sensation of having come home.

"Deal. Under one condition."

"What's that?"

"In exchange for all this extra work you're taking on, you let me fix dinner for you and Libby tonight."

"BEULAH," FRANK, her husband of forty years, said late Monday afternoon, "hate to be the one to tell you, but this time you've gone too far."

She snorted. "When it comes to keeping someone you love safe beside you, there's no such thing as too far."

Now Frank snorted.

"Hush up and finish what I asked you to do."

"You know this is going to send us straight to the poorhouse," he complained, stapling the pink-and-blue flyers she'd had printed at Bruce's Quick Copy and Car Wash. On each, she outlined the situation between her and her granddaughter's big-city uncle. And how, unless the man made significant changes—say, for instance, finding himself a suitable wife and remaining in IdaBelle Falls—Libby would be better off with her grandmother, thank you very much.

On the flyer's second page Beulah outlined a reward program of sorts. For each incident of documented genuine unkindness toward this outsider who'd come to steal her grandbaby, she'd pay double the money each business owner stood to lose by denying Travis Callahan their business.

Oh, she'd be the first to tell you it was dirty, but she didn't care. There was a method to her madness. Secretly, if she didn't get custody of Libby, Beulah had great respect for Kit. Now if while Travis was in town he happened to run into a few spots of trouble and he had to go to Kit for help...

Beulah grinned. Could she help it if nature took its course and those two ended up together? Yes, it would leave sweet Levi out in the cold, but if you asked her, he and Kit had always been more like brother and sister. Friends but no spark.

Marlene had once told her that Travis and Kit had been an item, so Beulah didn't see the harm in a little tinkering between Libby's godparents.

Beulah loved Libby with a ferocity that sometimes scared her. In fact, if Travis took little Libby away, Beulah wasn't sure she'd survive it. Or even if she'd want to survive, having already lost her only son.

Which was why, to assure her place in Libby's life, she loaded a care basket brimming with her granddaughter's favorite foods, then hustled toward the door.

"Now what're you doing?" her husband asked.

"Killing two birds with one stone." In other words, visiting her granddaughter and checking on the infant's caretaker.

Thirty minutes later Beulah pulled into the driveway of her son's former home, dead set on making progress on part of her mission—ensuring Travis was worthy of Libby and Kit!

Marching up the curving brick walk, past an overgrown yard, weed-choked garden and porch in need of paint, she was just about to call child welfare on her cell when a peek through the tall front windows netted her an unexpected sight. From the entry hall it was a straight shot to the kitchen, where Beulah saw Libby in her high chair, giggling, her chubby feet kicking as her uncle flew a baby spoon in circles just beyond her pinching reach. The air-conditioner made too much noise for Beulah to hear precisely what was going on, but she recognized her own grandchild's happy squeals clear enough.

Interesting.

Straightening her shoulders, she shifted the weighty basket from one hand to the other. As any grandmother would be, she was pleased Libby wasn't grief-stricken without her.

Anticipating getting her hands on that baby and daring to hope that if she didn't win custody she still might have a shot at getting Travis to stay in town, she rang the doorbell.

"What a nice surprise," the big-city cause of her every problem said a few minutes later, not looking the least bit pleased to see her.

Libby, on the other hand, cooed in his arms, holding out her stubby fingers.

"Here I am, baby girl. Mee Maw's right here," Beulah crooned, breathing in her precious baby scent.

"Made this for you," she said to Travis, passing him the basket containing still-warm pineapple upside-down cake, sliced ham, a jar of home-canned green beans, sun-warmed garden tomatoes and bread-and-butter pickles. "Thought you could use a little meat on your bones."

"Ah, thanks," he said.

"Don't mean to get in your business," she said as he closed the door, "but I thought you could use a break, and I sure could use some hugs." The last part she'd said in Libby's favorite high-pitched goofy voice, lifting the cutie high enough to blow a raspberry on her stomach. "Go on." She waved him off. "Take some time for yourself. Maybe go see what the child's godmother's up to. I'll care for our girl."

"TELL ME THIS IS JUST A bad dream," Travis said that night from behind the wheel to Libby, who was gumming a teething ring from her car seat on the first row of the Barnyard Babies Daycare van. The blaze-red van had cartoon cows and horses and chickens and ducks painted on the hood, back and sides. What he wouldn't give to be roaring along in his red Ferrari. He didn't drive it often. Most times he stuck to a staid black Mercedes sedan, but every once in a while he felt the need for speed. To find some desolate winding road and drive away the fears and doubts keeping him from being wholly satisfied with his life.

Libby, apparently perfectly content with their ob-noxious, oil-burning ride, happily gurgled.

"Just wait till you're a teenager," he said. "Then you won't be caught dead in this thing." It'd be good getting her home. To the intimacy of his penthouse, where he'd already hired a contractor and decorator to design a top-notch nursery and purchase myriad baby supplies.

In Chicago, his only staff was the housekeeper, and he and Libby would get to know each other— the way real family should. That Gary's mom was trying to steal the infant from him wasn't even a factor. He wouldn't allow even the suspicion of defeat to enter his head.

Pulling onto Crabapple Lane, Travis found the small white house with a pink flamingo family in the front, as Kit had described. The quintuplet of birds was tacky, but set in a field of pink impatiens, they somehow fit the country-style cottage with its cozy gingerbread-encrusted front porch and forest-green shutters.

As welcoming as the place was, it did have one fatal flaw—Levi's pickup parked alongside Kit's beige Honda.

Travis hadn't realized how much he'd been looking forward to the night alone with Kit until discovering they'd be chaperoned by her fiancé.

"You found it," Libby's godmother said, bounding out the front door and across the fragrant freshly mowed lawn. "Have any trouble?"

"Nope," he said, plucking Libby from her seat. "Your directions were great. What smells so good?" he asked, Libby cradled to his chest as he shut the van door. The air was filled with the sweet, smoky scent of barbecue that made his stomach rumble. He was getting tired of bologna sandwiches. Which reminded him—in the morning, he'd have to head to the grocery store. In the meantime, would it be asking too much for Kit to cook up a mess of barbecued ribs?

"Levi's a wiz with the grill. He's making ribs. His specialty."

While she held out her arms to take Libby, and while Travis passed off the infant to her, struggling to ignore the blinding bolt of awareness just being near her evoked, he took a stab at reminding himself he was a grown-up. Just because Levi had made dinner instead of Kit wasn't the cause of Travis's sudden loss of appetite.

"Has Libby eaten yet?"

"No. I planned on just mashing up some of whatever you'd fixed. And if she doesn't like that, I've got pureed pork chops, peas and homemade applesauce Beulah made her." He patted the diaper bag hanging from his right shoulder.

"Beulah? She came over again?"

"Yep."

"Was it any better than the last time?" she asked, leading him deeper into her comfortable shabby-chic home.

"Surprisingly not half-bad. More in the realm of your typical filling as opposed to a root canal."

Kit laughed.

"Plus, Libby clearly adores her. While they

played, I got work done. It was a win-win for everyone. Shocked the you-know-what out of me."

Kit's smile filled Travis with asinine pride. "I'm glad you came. This'll be fun. We got off to a rocky start, but tonight we'll start a new chapter as not only business partners but, I hope, friends." She led the way inside, making kissy noises to the baby while Libby fisted her hair.

Like a lost dog, Travis trailed after her, dreading the moment Levi appeared, knowing it was inevitable and therefore slipping on his corporate mask. What was it about Kit that brought on a mile-long possessive streak?

The inside of her house was every bit as welcoming and quirky as the outside. Somehow she'd managed to take a hodgepodge of weary case goods and upholstered pieces and had shaped them into a comfortable home tinted in varying shades of green, gold and cream. The entry hall alone of his family home was the size of her entire house, yet for all its elegance and priceless sculptures and art, it didn't hold half the warmth of Kit's simple abode.

"Let me take that," she said, reaching for the diaper bag.

"I see you're a big fan of adventure novels." He gestured toward a simple oak shelf bursting with titles of authors he'd also read.

"Guilty." She kissed the crown of Libby's head. "I love the feeling of embarking on a big adventure. You know, finding a little treasure, then saving the world."

She stroked the infant's hair for a moment, then looked to him, meeting his gaze with unexpected intensity. "That's what you're doing here, you know— saving Libby's world. With Beulah, she'd be all right, but it just wouldn't be the same. With you, she stands the chance of growing up with a real dad."

"Now all she needs is a mom, huh?" Travis winked.

"You asking me to apply for the job?" Kit asked, a playful twinkle lighting her eyes.

"Mmm…that depends," he teased right back. "I'll have to sample your cooking first. After all, a kid needs lots of good home cooking."

"Problem," she pointed out.

"What's that?"

"Levi's doing all the cooking tonight. All I did was make a batch of sweet tea and predinner snacks."

"Sorry. Deal's off." They both grinned, and even Libby let loose with a smiling gurgle, and for a split second, right up until Levi came strolling in, they'd felt like a unit—an almost family. That is, if they'd known each other longer than a couple days and that forever-ago hot summer.

"Hey, Travis," Levi said with a hearty pat to his back. "Hope you're hungry, 'cause I've got a mess of ribs out there on the grill."

"Sure am," Travis said.

"Great. Come on out and we can talk guy stuff over cold ones." He handed Travis a beer bottle.

Travis would rather have had scotch but twisted the top off and gulped.

"I see you whipped up a batch of that potato salad I love," Levi said, slipping his arm around Kit's waist, then planting a big, fat kiss to her inviting lips. "I'm touched you remembered it's my favorite."

Travis's stomach clenched.

"Why else do you think I made it?" she asked in one of those soft lover's voices that made Travis feel like a voyeur to overhear.

Libby still in Kit's arms, they kissed.

Travis cleared his throat. "Um, I'm feeling like a third wheel here. There anything you two need me to do in the kitchen or with the grill?"

Laughing, looking so at ease in Levi's arms Travis wanted to hurl, Kit said, "You're our honored guest. How about you find a seat out on the patio, then I'll bring you a plate of my famous hot wings."

Nice.

Travis scowled. Levi got hot kisses and all Travis would be getting was jacked-up poultry.

TWO HOURS LATER DINNER was blessedly over and Travis had to begrudgingly admit to having enjoyed the meal. Levi and Kit were excellent cooks. Leading him to wonder what he was good at other than buy-outs and mergers. And why, when he'd once been proud of that fact, did it now fill him with uncertainty? Why did he want to be the one grilling ribs that made Kit groan after taking her first delicious bite?

"This has been great," Levi said with a broad yawn

over the sound of crickets and faint country music spilling onto the patio through Kit's screen door. It'd rained that afternoon, reducing the temperature to a not just bearable but actually pleasant eighty degrees. "But I've gotta be up with the roosters. We start our annual lawn-mower sale in the morning."

"I forgot about that," Kit said. "Good luck."

They were back to kissing.

Travis was back to wishing he could zap himself to another planet.

"Guess Libby and I should get going, too," he said, already pushing his chair back to grab Libby from her makeshift crib of a pile of blankets and a pillow barrier on the living room floor. He was thrilled for the opportunity to leave yet at the same time wishing he could stay here instead of heading back to Marlene and Gary's empty-feeling house.

"I hate it that you're both leaving so soon," she said. "But I guess we all have to be up early."

"Let me at least help with the dishes," Levi said, unwittingly making Travis feel like an inconsiderate jerk for not having asked first.

"That's okay," Kit said. "We pretty much tackled the worst of the damage as we went along."

"Sure?" he asked again.

She nodded.

He cupped his hands around her shoulders, drawing her in for a serious kiss. A kiss that left no question that Levi was staking his claim.

Trying to be a gentleman about the awkward situation, Travis looked away, taking the half-empty blackberry pie plate from the redwood patio table and carrying it inside. In the kitchen he rummaged through a few drawers for plastic wrap.

Levi started up his truck, then came a whiff of exhaust as he pulled away and Kit walked in through the back door.

"That was really nice," she said. "I'm so glad you could come."

"Sure," he said, fitting the wrap around the pie.

"You don't have to do that."

"I know." *But I want to. I want to show you I'm every bit as good as Levi—better, even if I've never manned a grill.* Why he felt this compulsion he wasn't sure. Guilt for the way things had been left between them when there'd been a them?

"Mmm," she said, hugging herself, gazing toward the ceiling with a melancholy smile. "Levi and I used to double date with your sister and Gary all the time. We'll have to fix you up with someone so next time you're over there will be an equal number of us at the table."

"We had Libby."

"You know what I mean," she said, swatting him with a dish towel. "We need a woman for you. There were a couple times tonight I got the feeling you were lonely."

"Me?" He laughed, turning on the hot water, then putting the drain plug in the sink and squirting in green dishwashing liquid. Funny how he'd never once in his life washed dishes before coming here, yet now he did them at least a half dozen times a day. Even odder, he liked doing them. Liked the feel of immersing his hands in the warm, sudsy water. Crazy as it might seem, it was comforting, the normalcy of it. "I've got all I can handle with a pint-size girl."

"Still," she said, easing up beside him, taking the plate he'd just washed to rinse, then dry. "I don't see what it'd hurt for you to go out on one little date. What about Chrissy?" she asked with a brazen wink. "I happen to have it on good authority that she thinks you're a grade-A prime piece of meat."

Travis nearly choked.

"Thanks, but no thanks," he said. "I'm good on my own." *But I'd be better with you.*

Where the thought had come from he didn't know. Probably that mingling with Kit's honeysuckle, smoky scent was the light fragrance of the real deal climbing a trellis outside the open windows. A light breeze fluttered the gauzy curtains.

"You don't find Chrissy attractive?"

"Did I say that?" he snapped, bored with the topic.

"No, but—"

"Really, it's nothing personal," he said, handing her the last of the plates, wishing their warm, slick fingers hadn't brushed, igniting a hunger deep in his belly that had nothing to with ribs and everything to do with her lips. "Chrissy's a great girl. I'm just not—"

"Over Marlene?"

"Exactly," he said, glad for the out, even if it was a lie. Yes, he was still devastated over his sister's passing, but that wasn't the real reason why he didn't want to date his coworker. That stemmed more from the woman standing beside him.

"Before you go," she said, flitting off to the fridge, "let me fix you a plate of leftovers."

"Thanks. That sounds good for breakfast."

While she fixed his plate, he gathered Libby's gear, which even in their brief stay had magically scattered. Finished, he returned to the kitchen, only to find Kit no longer there. "Kit?"

"Out here!" she called from the patio.

He stepped outside, back into the night noisy with the hum of cicadas and two or three crickets chirping in the bushes. Somewhere off in the darkness a whip-poor-will sang its lonely song.

Whip-poor-will.

Whip-poor-will.

His hostess sat at the table, resting her feet on one of the neighboring fat-cushioned chairs. She'd leaned her head against the chair's back, exposing her elegant throat to the flicker of citronella candles. "It's a beautiful night, isn't it?"

He couldn't have given a flip about the night. All he had eyes for was her. She'd worn a cream-colored sundress that looked great with her tan. Now she'd hiked it midway up her thighs and slipped her gold-toned sandals off, wriggling red-tipped toes.

Smiling, she said, "Is there any better feeling in the world than taking off your shoes?"

Chuckling, drawing out the chair beside her and taking a seat, he said, "I can think of a few things I'd rather feel."

"All right," she said, a challenge behind her smile, the hair she'd released from its ponytail caressing her cheeks. "Name them."

"In current company?" he asked, trying for a shocked expression. "I might offend your tender ears."

"Try me," she goaded, facing him straight on.

"All right—a clean one would be taking off my tie."

"Lame." After an exaggerated yawn, she said, "I thought you were going to shock me."

"If it's shock you want…" He helped himself to a sip of her iced tea, seeing how he'd long since washed his glass. "I like those last few seconds leading up to a kiss. Mingling the heat of each other's breath."

Fanning herself, cheeks reddening even in the gloom, she said, "'Kay. You win."

"How 'bout you?" he teased. "You're a big girl. Anything naughty you particularly enjoy?"

"We shouldn't be having this discussion," she said.

"Who says? You see any conduct police?"

"No, but…" She ran the pad of her thumb through the condensation on her glass. Without much effort, Travis wondered what other contrasts might she enjoy. Maybe an ice cube swirled atop sensitive places? "You daring me to come up with something even more scandalous?"

Flashing her a half grin, he shrugged. "You wanna consider it a dare, I don't have a problem with it. Come on, give me your best shot."

"Okay," she said after a hitched breath, licking her lips. "I like it when—" Blushing all the more, she leaned close to whisper the last part in his ear in a breathy rush. Instantly hard, instantly wanting to try the trick himself, he shifted in his seat.

"Damn, woman," he couldn't help but tease, taking inordinate pride in the memory of her having first tried that trick with him. "Your momma know you talk about such things?"

"Fortunately, no," she said, landing a light swat to his arm.

"Good. Filth like that just might land her in the E.R."

"Me, filthy?" She poked his ribs. "How's what I said any worse than your admission?"

"I was just talking generalities. You gave specifics."

"So?" She sipped tea from the same side of her glass his lips had just moments earlier touched. "Like you said…I'm a big girl. Maybe I have a few needs."

A secret smile tugging the corners of her ripe, gorgeous lips, an irrational fury streaked through Travis upon the realization that it was Levi fulfilling those needs.

"I, uh, better go," he said, pushing back his chair.

"What's the matter? Conversation too hot?" She winked.

"As a matter of fact," he said, standing, then planting a chaste kiss to her cheek. "Seeing how you're practically a married woman—yes. See you in the morning?"

"Looking forward to it. Want me to help you out with Libby?"

"Nope." *What I want to do is imagine you all sudsy and naked in a hot bath, waiting for me to join you.*

Sharply exhaling, shaking his head at his latest inappropriate thought, Travis cast Kit one last smile, then scooped up his snoozing niece and her diaper bag, showing himself out the door.

Only after he'd gotten a good five miles down the road did he relax. And then, for the first time since landing back in IdaBelle Falls, he genuinely laughed.

"If I didn't know better," he grumbled, halfway eyeing the heavens, "Marlene Callahan-Redding, I'd swear you were up there looking down on me, somehow manipulating this whole thing. Making me want a woman I can't have."

Though the realist in him knew the North Star hadn't winked at him, the sliver of a closet romantic in him knew full well it had.

Chapter Seven

After tossing and turning for a good thirty minutes, Kit finally got up and found the latest James Rollins novel she'd been saving for the weekend. No way was she going to dive into a romance considering that Travis had somehow gotten her all hot and bothered without so much as a single touch or kiss.

Which was nuts.

She was engaged to Levi. She'd been dating him for the past three years. He was a warm and funny and wonderfully considerate man she knew full well she'd one day marry. So how come it wasn't his hands she imagined kneading her swollen and achy breasts? How come when she'd playfully whispered that secret to Travis, it'd sparked guilty past images of him she couldn't banish from her mind? Yes, they'd once been lovers, but just because they'd shared a hot past didn't mean that in the future they'd be anything more than friends. Especially when Travis had made it clear he didn't plan to stay in IdaBelle Falls after the hearing.

The only reason she felt close to him was that he was Marlene's brother. Because of their love for her, they shared a special bond. Levi had known Marlene, but he certainly hadn't loved her.

Despite the evening's awkward end, it had started awfully nice. Levi and Travis had gotten along well. And Libby, as always, had been a doll. Kit was disappointed that Travis had flat-out rejected her idea of his dating Chrissy, but maybe he was right in that it was too soon for him to even be thinking of dating.

Why, then, had he seemed so comfortable sharing all that flirty adult talk with you?

Argh. After not even managing to get through the first page of the novel she'd anticipated since finishing the author's last book, Kit pushed up from the sofa and marched to the bathroom. What she needed was a long soak to clear her mind and get her ready for a good night's sleep.

Yeah, right, she thought, turning the porcelain taps and adjusting the water. Who was she trying to kid? What she really planned on doing was relieving the tension Travis Callahan had brought on simply by sitting across the table from her and flashing his devil-may-care, sexy-as-hell grin.

What kind of messed-up woman did that make her? She was in love with Levi, right? The man she planned to marry. Assuming that was true, then how come ever since Travis had returned to town just a few days earlier, her life had felt upside down?

"WHAT DO YOU MEAN YOU can't get someone out here to deliver groceries?" Travis barked Tuesday morning into the daycare's loft phone. Damn sick and tired of getting the same negative response from every business in town—from Kountry Klean Maid Service to Big Steve's Lawn Care to Harson's Heating and Air, who he'd phoned in hopes of getting central heat and AC installed so the house wouldn't have cold and hot spots, which were not only uncomfortable to him but couldn't be healthy for Libby.

"I'm sorry, sir," the Grab & Bag's manager said, "but delivery's just not a service we offer."

Sighing and shoving his hand through his hair, Travis said, "I'm offering a hundred bucks over whatever it actually costs just to refill the pantry."

"Again, sir, while I appreciate the offer, she—I mean, we, I mean, well, it's just not possible."

"Which *she* would we be talking about?" Straightening in Marlene's rickety wood desk chair, it occurred to Travis that in a town the size of IdaBelle Falls the *she* the manager had mentioned must be Beulah. Why, beyond pure spite, she'd want to deny him and her granddaughter food was beyond him, but if she was behind the store's failure to help, then fine. He'd tackle grocery shopping on his own.

Even so, he would like to know definitively if his sister's mother-in-law was playing dirty. Might be useful in court. "I'm hearing an awful lot of silence. Is there some reason you don't want me to know who this mystery woman is?"

The teen cleared his throat "I'm not at liberty to say, but if you'd like to speak to our general manager, I'm sure he'd be happy to—"

"Won't be necessary. Thanks." Travis hung up, then fought the need to roar in frustration. Obviously this bizarre small town was circling wagons around a woman they wanted to protect.

But why? Did they like and respect Beulah to that degree? Or did she hold power over them and they were scared of her?

Footsteps sounded on the stairs, which he recognized as Kit's—she had a unique rhythm as she walked. A never-rushed sashay.

The exotic gait might've been a turn-on if they were more than friends, but he certainly wasn't in the market for female companionship and she was engaged, so—

"What's got your panties in a wad?" she teased, descending into her own red floral desk chair and swirling to face him.

"I wear boxers," he said, trying to hold back an annoyed growl.

"*Excuuuuse* me," she said with a pretty grin that put the nail on the coffin of his crappy mood.

What was it with her always being so chipper? "Don't you ever have down moments?"

"Sure. Don't we all? I just don't see the need to bring everyone else down around me."

"That's what I'm doing?" he asked, kneading his aching forehead. "Bringing you down?"

"Four-year-old Kyle did ask what that grumpy man was doing upstairs. And if you need help fighting bad guys."

"Ha!" He snorted. "More like a bad woman. How is it possible that Beulah single-handedly managed to get every service in town to turn away my business? At any price. What is it about this Hicksville place that doesn't respond to—"

"First off," she began, her lips pressed in an un- mistakable frown, "our lovely town does not take kindly to outsiders referring to it as *Hicksville*. Second, Beulah's a God-fearing woman and would never deliberately sabotage you." She blanched as if the very word had been distasteful on her tongue. "Third, why do you even need all these other folks doing things for you? You're a big, strong man, Travis Callahan. Would it kill you to do your own cooking or cleaning or lawn care?"

Yes, actually, it quite possibly could kill him! But out of pure dumb pride, he'd never tell her he hadn't done any of the tasks she mentioned in years. Growing up, his only chore had been excelling at school.

"Well?" she asked again. "Would it technically kill you to perform manual labor?"

"Mind your own business," he said, hating his coarse tone but unwilling to bend on the issue. There had to be someone in this town who was willing to stand up to Beulah Redding.

"Whether I like it or not," Kit said, scooting

toward him in her chair like one of the kids she was supposed to be watching, "you are my business."

"How's that?" he asked, refusing to meet her gaze even though he knew by the hum setting off alarms in his already overloaded system that she'd nestled her closed legs in between his before planting her hands on the arms of his chair.

"On her deathbed, your sister asked me to watch out for you. To help you see there's more to life than working at a job you reportedly don't even like."

He rolled his eyes. "Mowing is magically supposed to make me a better person?"

"Not a better person, a more rounded one. Happier. Based on your last statement, I'm going to assume you've never mowed a lawn. Yes, sometimes it's a hassle, but to some people it's like giving a haircut to your little corner of the world. The freshly shorn grass smells so good, all fresh and springy, and then you sit on the front porch swing with a sweet tea, surveying a job well done. You might be tired, but it's a good tired. A kind of tired you've never before felt."

He rolled his eyes.

She patted his knees. Grinned. "Mark my words, by the time you win your battle against Beulah, you'll never want to leave IdaBelle Falls."

"Sorry to burst your bubble," he said, covering her hands with his, "but you're wrong." Yes, one stupid, sappy summer he'd seen this place—Kit herself—as home. But now both were nothing but an ever-growing pain in his butt.

"BEULAH," FRANK SAID Tuesday evening, slipping off his reading glasses to shoot his wife a dirty look.

"Yes, dear?" Acting the innocent, she looked up from the pink booties she'd been knitting to match the pink cape and hat she was making Libby for Christmas.

"Do you have any idea how much this scheme of yours is costing?" He sat at the living room's rolltop desk, overwhelmed by bills. Yes, even by big-city standards, they were a wealthy family, but at the rate money had been flying out the door, he wasn't sure they'd have enough in their retirement savings to last another month, let alone, God willing, the next twenty years.

"I don't care what it costs," she said. "I want my baby home."

"Has it ever occurred to you that we've already raised our child? That Libby might be better off being raised by an uncle closer to her age?"

Pfft. "A bachelor uncle who'll no doubt carry on with a string of bleached-hair floozies." Unless he opened his eyes wide enough to see Kit and the amazing life right here in IdaBelle Falls they could share.

"Beulah Redding, how can you sit there all high and mighty, claiming you've never once had salon-assisted hair coloring? You don't watch those fibs of yours, God's not gonna let you through the church doors come Sunday morning."

"Mark my words," she said with a brazen wink, pointing her knitting needle at him. "God's on my side."

"You're wrong," he said. "If he's any kind of God

at all, he's on Libby's side—and doing whatever's best for her pint-size soul."

"Speaking of which," she said, "it's high time I gave my sweet angel another visit. Care to tag along?"

"BEULAH!" KIT SANG OUT that evening from the day-care's play yard. Their last client had gone home, and while Travis was picking up toys, she disinfected them. Though she adored her job, this had always been her favorite part of the day, when quiet reigned and long shadows cooled golden sun. The baby lounged on a blanket spread on the grass, buzzing raspberries at a ladybug who'd dared invade her turf. "If you're looking for Libby, she's over here!"

"Honest to Pete," Beulah said, slamming the door on her red Caddie, huffing her way across the gravel drive. "Couldn't y'all have spared a thought for distance when designing this place?"

"Sorry," Kit said. "Considering our typical client is three and we'd like them to burn off as much excess energy as possible before entering the premises, we kind of like wide-open spaces."

Harrumph was Beulah's answer.

"You didn't happen to bring any more of that pineapple upside-down cake?" Travis asked, wiping sweat from his brow with the sleeve of a used-to-be-white-now-gray oxford.

"Depends," Marlene's mother-in-law said. "If I give you more cake, you gonna testify to the judge that I'm the better cook?"

"Beulah!" Kit said. "You're using your famous cake for blackmail?"

Making a beeline for Libby, the older woman smiled. "Can I help it if the judge recognizes advanced cooking skills?" Scooping the infant into her arms, Mercenary Granny turned all sweetness and sunshine, softening her voice to a silly coo. "There's my sweet sugar baby. Give me love."

Enraptured, Libby burst into giggles. As did Beulah.

Kit glanced Travis's way to find him scowling.

Poor guy. It had to be hard enough losing his sister. The last thing he needed on top of that still-raw pain was a drawn out custody battle.

"I was wondering," Beulah said, Libby still tucked to her ample bosom, "if I could please take this angel with me to church choir practice? It's been ages since my girls have seen her, and in exchange," she said to Travis, "I've got two cakes and a great big pan of homemade chicken and dumplings guaranteed to make you sit up and cry for your momma."

Eyes narrowed, Travis said, "And I suppose you've got some hidden camera in the kitchen, so you can show this feasting to the judge?"

"Why, I never," she said, hand to her chest, grinning down at Libby. "Have you ever been so insulted in all your days?"

The baby grinned.

"Beulah," Kit said, "you just admitted to using cake for evil. Why would you now turn around and use it for good?"

"What's wrong with me wanting to show off my granddaughter? In the process, you two get a free meal with all the trimmings. I'll have Libby home before bedtime."

"What do you think?" Travis asked, spilling his last batch of toys onto the picnic table.

Kit groaned. "Seeing all the work we have left to do, I vote for the free meal."

"Of course you do," Beulah said. "Now you two just do whatever it is you do around here, and Libby and I will put the food in the fridge and then be on our way. Have fun, y'all!"

Thirty minutes later, seated at Marlene and Gary's leaning metal kitchen table, three begging dogs as their audience, Kit said, "I hate to even think about it, but maybe you've been right all along and Beulah's up to no good. But her meal's so delicious it's like some form of hypnosis."

"Ditto," her companion said, downing another creamy bite, then doling out one bite each for the dogs.

"If this was a ploy," Kit asked, rolling her eyes at Mr. Softy, "what's her motive?"

"Obviously to make me look bad. But here's the way I see it—" he set down his fork to swig Beulah's famous sweet tea "—how bad a guy can I be if I give the two some time together?"

"Good point."

Kit's cell phone came alive with a country ringtone Levi had picked to identify his calls.

"Excuse me," she said, hopping up to grab it from her purse, which she'd set on the counter.

"Go for it," Travis said. "One of us might as well have fun." He winked.

She swatted. "Hey, what's up?"

"Have dinner yet?"

She eyed the table. "Actually…"

"Great. If you have, then I won't feel bad about hanging with the guys down at the Eight Ball. Finch's heartbroken over Sheila dumping him for the third time, so we figured on cheering him up."

"Sure," she said, oddly relieved that her fiancé had plans. "Take your time."

"Want me to swing by your place when we're done?"

"No," she said, unable to break her stare on the most fascinating spot on Travis's newly tanned neck. "It'll be late. You just go on home. I'll see you sometime tomorrow."

Travis asked, "This mean I get you all to myself?"

Giving him a dirty look, Kit flipped her phone shut.

"Sorry. Your man's a loud talker. It's a quiet kitchen. I couldn't help but overhear. Trouble in paradise?"

"No." At least she'd never had a troubled heart until Travis jetted back into town—not that there even was a problem now. Just that the potential for it seemed to skyrocket whenever she and Travis were in the same room.

"Then what's with that guilty grin and the hair

twirling? Are you jazzed about spending the evening with me and my mutts but afraid to admit it?"

"I'm not hair twirling," she said, landing another swat to his nearest shoulder. "And for your information, I feel guilty spending time with you because—"

"Yes? I'm waiting."

Fanning suddenly red cheeks, she grinned. To coin Beulah's favorite catchall, honest to Pete! Was it any of his business why she found herself enjoying his company more and more? Especially since she didn't have a clue what it was about his devilish charm that made him so darned irresistible, just that she was powerless to deny it.

Chapter Eight

Thursday, a couple hours since the last pint-size day-care client had left for the day, Travis was taking the trash out to the big, smelly green bin in the shed when Cocoa slipped out the door after him.

She bounded after something, but the grass around the house was so tall, if it hadn't been for her high-pitched barks, he'd have thought the dog had vanished.

Levi had mowed the lawn around the barn's parking area and the children's play yard, but he hadn't touched the area around the house, so where a lawn used to be now stood a two-foot-tall field. None of the daycare's customers had said anything, but the already rundown house had become a down-right embarrassment. And seeing how no amount of bribes seemed to be getting Travis anywhere with the local landscape folks, it looked as though he'd have to tackle the job on his own—no problem, right?

Ha! After getting Libby fed, bathed and in her crib for the night, he strapped her monitor to the waistband of his khaki cargo shorts, then marched out to the shed to find a lawn mower.

In the gloomy shed Travis found one just fine, but maneuvering it outside past the fifty-pound bag of dry dog food he'd purchased at the feed store was no easy feat. Still, once he'd accomplished that and the mower sat squarely on the shed's concrete surround, he found the pull handle and gave it a tug.

Nothing happened.

He did it again and again until sweat beaded between his shoulder blades and he was tugging up the hem of his black T-shirt to wipe his brow.

Okay, so now what?

He searched the mower's body for starting instructions, then the shed for a mower manual, but bombed both missions.

He could just go buy a new mower—after all, Levi's store was having a sale. But the hardware store was closed. And by the time he got Libby dressed, out to the van and to the nearest Wal-Mart— an hour away—it'd be closed, too.

Sure, he could put mowing off one more day, but dammit, he wanted the job done. Most of all he wanted the satisfaction of seeing the look on Kit's face when she pulled up in the morning and saw it.

Inspiration struck.

Levi might not have his store open, but surely he'd have a few tips as to how to go about starting this unruly mowing beast.

Marching inside, Travis unearthed a phone book from a pile of unread newspapers. Lucky for him, small-town folk didn't see the need for unlisted numbers, and a second later he was dialing Levi's number.

Only, a woman answered. "Kit?"

"Travis?"

"Hey, how are you?"

"So then it is you?" she asked. "Calling my fiancé?" Her smile shone through her voice. "Curious. Most curious."

"How so? I'm a man. Why would it be odd for me to want to speak with someone other than women and preschoolers?"

"There's Lincoln," she said with a laugh. "He's in second grade."

"Ha-ha," Travis said in a deadpan tone. "Levi around?"

"Maybe. Depends on what you want with him. This was supposed to have been a romantic evening—just the two of us."

He sighed. "Is he there or not? I promise, I'm only after a second of his time."

"Well, in that case…" The clunk of her setting down the phone as well as her continued chuckle came over the line.

Stupid, he thought with a thorough rub of his jaw. That's what calling Levi had been.

Had he been a wise man, not so damned impatient to prove his competency to all these local yokels—

Kit—he would've waited till morning to purchase a new machine.

"Travis," Levi said in a booming voice. "How's it hanging, bud? What can I do for you?"

Still recovering from the volume of Kit's future groom's voice, Travis said, "I, ah, have a situation I wonder if you could help with."

"Love to if I can. Shoot."

Travis haltingly explained his mower woes, then Levi told him about a rubbery-feeling button he had to press a few times, after which, the beast should start right up.

"Thanks," Travis said, seeing some of what Kit found attractive in the guy. Levi could've belittled Travis for not knowing something so basic to most men. Instead, he'd patiently explained what the problem may be, then even offered to come right over if it still didn't start. Knowing how furious Kit would be if he were responsible for lousing up her big date, Travis politely declined the offer.

After hanging up, Travis headed upstairs for a peek at Libby, all three dogs clacking after him.

Knowing the whole town was against him, save two people who were no doubt currently in each other's arms, had left him feeling lonely. Why, he couldn't fathom. He could've called Chrissy for company, but he didn't want her finding more in the gesture than the offer of friendship it would've been.

Not that he didn't think she was a cute girl.

Just not the girl for him.

Not that he was even looking for a girl.

Just that—oh, hell.

To get his mind off the constantly rolling footage of Kit and Levi engaging in all manner of adult entertainment, he lightly stroked Libby's downy-soft hair, then, in fading daylight, headed back outside to wrestle with the monster otherwise known as the lawn mower.

"Wow," Kit said with a whistle the next morning, spotting Travis reading to the children. "The yard looks great. Who'd you find to mow it?"

"You're looking at him," Travis said.

"No way."

"Do you mind?" he said, bristling, turning the big, colorful page. "We're right in the middle of a key scene here."

"Oh, by all means," she said. "Don't let me interrupt."

"What's wrong with him?" Kit asked Chrissy, who was busy making the midmorning snack of apple slices, peanut butter and cranberry juice.

"Beats me. He's been great with the kids all morning but otherwise a real bear."

"Thanks for the heads-up," Kit said. "Has the new girl gotten here yet?"

"Yeah. She's upstairs filling out paperwork."

"Great. Thanks." Kit headed that way.

Hard to believe that in the few days since Travis had started advertising they'd already had enough new enrollments to warrant hiring help.

"Oh, hi, Mrs. Petty," the new girl, Stephanie, called over her shoulder from Marlene's desk. The short-haired brunette with more energy than five toddlers put together was a great find. The twenty-two-year-old was fresh out of the University of Arkansas with a primary education degree. She'd grown up in the area and was now hoping for a teaching position at IdaBelle Falls Elementary, but seeing how one had yet to crop up, she was a perfect fit for the daycare. "Thanks again for the job."

"Thank you," Kit said. "We're lucky to have you. And for the record, Levi and I aren't married."

"Seriously?" The girl's eyebrows shot up. "I swear I saw your wedding announcement in the paper."

"Nope. Must've been our engagement notice," Kit said, tidying papers on her desk. Before Travis had come back to town, the question would've been cause for frustration as she'd been ready to set a wedding date—and regularly let Levi know—for the past year, but Levi wasn't in a hurry. He said it was because he wanted an ample nest egg set aside. But between them they'd saved a tidy chunk of change, so now what was the holdup? Kit, as the only child of parents who'd both worked long hours and now spent the majority of their time traveling in their RV, very much looked forward to having a family all her own. All of which made it all the more puzzling why at the moment marrying Levi seemed to be the furthest thing from her mind.

What was on her mind? Hanging with Travis.

Caring for Libby. Neither of which struck her as pastimes moving her closer to her marriage goal.

"Well," her new employee said, "it'll be nice when you two do finally get hitched. I'm sure you'll be over-the-moon happy. He's just about the sweetest thing I've ever seen."

Not sure what to say, especially in light of the dud of an evening she and Levi had just had, Kit smiled.

"I sure could use a good man," the girl said, a wistful smile lighting her pretty features. "Seems like in college I had at least one date every weekend, but ever since moving back here my social life's a disaster."

"Oh?" Seeing the potted ivy on her desk needed watering, Kit used the remains of yesterday's bottled water to give it a dowsing.

"What do you know about Travis?" Stephanie asked. "I mean, he's obviously a hunk, but is he available?"

Crap! Can you say soggy mess? Kit had watered the ivy all right, along with everything else on her desk. As much as she liked Stephanie, a flash of irritation soured her stomach. This was a daycare she was running, not a meat market!

Oh, yeah? Hadn't it been only a few days earlier she'd been willing to help send Travis and Chrissy on a date? What was the problem with him and Steph?

Frowning, Kit knew full well what the problem was—old-fashioned jealousy. Only, seeing how she was engaged to Levi, shouldn't it be high time for her to release her first love?

"I'll help," Stephanie said, yanking tissues from a box on the desk's dry side to dab at the sprawling ooze.

"Thanks." Kit strove to regain composure she wasn't even sure why she'd lost. Moments earlier she'd been in a great mood. How come the mere mention of Travis moving on with his life had made a mess of not just her desk but her insides?

Finished with the worst of the cleanup, Stephanie persisted. "Well? Is Travis single? If so, I might need to pay a little more attention to my hair and makeup in the mornings."

"Um…" Kit cleared her throat. "He is, uh, single. But we have a strict company policy against employee fraternization." *Liar!* "You know how it is. We wouldn't want the children to be emotionally scarred by catching their teachers in a compromising position."

Stephanie giggled. "Oh, I'd never do anything like that. I mean—that is, if he even wanted to go out. We'd keep our work relationship strictly professional."

"All the same," Kit said, scooping three pens from her cluttered desk, then slamming them into a side drawer. "I'll have to insist you keep your relationship with all fellow employees strictly professional."

"O-okay," the girl said. "Sorry. I didn't mean to cause trouble."

"No trouble." Kit forced a smile. "Just trying to run a tight ship."

Kit remained upstairs until Stephanie finished her paperwork, then gave her a tour of the operation. By the time she'd finished, it was the children's nap time, and she encouraged Chrissy and Stephanie to share lunch on the play yard picnic table. The overcast day was cool, making it, for once, actually inviting to be outdoors.

The two women took Kit up on her invitation, leaving her on her own in the kitchen, microwaving leftovers of Levi's spaghetti dinner. Travis was in the loft, ticking away on Marlene's computer keyboard. He was supposed to have had a vast array of computer equipment and office furniture delivered to the house, but it was as slow in arriving as he'd been in thawing his icy mood.

When the microwave dinged, announcing the completion of her meal, she took it and a Coke upstairs, along with a monitor that would alert her if any of her cherubs woke prematurely.

At her desk, she'd planned on Web-surfing for a while. Maybe arrange a dream tropical honeymoon in the unlikely event she found a pot of gold or won the lottery, then also happened to get married. Trouble was, her computer had frozen, and the only way to get the ancient model unfrozen was to turn it off, then start it again. Grumbling, trying to ignore Travis while her computer did its thing, she dug into her lunch, only to find it still cold in the center.

Cursing under her breath, she shoved back her chair to heat her food more, only the chair's front wheels caught in the rag rug, sending her and the plate flying.

While she did more cursing, Travis said, "Oops."

To his credit, after his less-than-helpful sarcastic comment, he did at least join her on the floor in scooping up the mess.

"What's your problem?" she said, on her knees beside him, close enough to feel his heat.

"My problem?" He laughed. "To everyone but the kids you've been Lil' Miss Crabby all day."

"Excuse me?" Stunned he would suggest she'd been the grumpy one, she sat back on her haunches, fistfuls of spaghetti in her hands. "I've been perfectly polite."

He snorted. "For a testy wildebeest."

"Oh—like you've been Mr. Sunshine?"

"I think so."

"You weren't so polite when I first walked in this morning, barking at me not to interrupt your story."

"Sorry," he said. "I was sore. Yard work's a bitch."

"Language," she snapped, trying to grapple to her feet without touching her spaghetti-covered hands to any still-clean surface. He was sore. At least that explained his short fuse. How about hers? She refused to believe it had anything to do with Stephanie's question and that quickly after Kit realized that ever since Travis had returned, her carefully planned life mirrored her overturned spaghetti.

"Language?" He rolled his eyes. "Everyone's sleeping."

"Still. While working in a child-filled environment, you should always maintain a certain decorum."

"Which would include not *fraternizing* with other employees?"

"Where'd you hear that?" she asked, hoping fire flashed from her eyes as she continued her clamber to her feet.

Grinning, he shrugged. "Office gossip travels."

"Stephanie told you?" she asked, slipping on a glop of wet noodles.

Seeing how he'd kept one hand clean to maneuver, Travis was already on his feet helping steady her on hers. Only, he also grabbed her with his one meat-sauce-covered hand and smeared a path from her forearm to her fingers. At first, the sensation was disgusting, but then, as the sauce that was still warm mingled with body heat, the whole thing became alarmingly erotic—in a bizarre preschool-lunch-hour sort of way.

"I, um, didn't mean to get you all messy," he said, releasing her as abruptly as he'd taken her hand. He followed his words with a funny heated look, as if he'd been about to say something but changed his mind.

"Th-that's okay," she said. "I did a great job of messing myself."

"Come on," he said, his hand now back on her forearm, radiating swirls of wandering heat. "Let's get you cleaned up."

Strictly in the event her sneaker soles were slick, Kit held Travis's hand down the stairs. At the sink, she let him use his clean hand to reach for the soap bottle, squirting some onto her hands. Beneath warm, flowing water, he washed her hands and forearms as gently as he would have Libby's. Only, the sizzling awareness between them was far from paternal.

"Thanks," she said when he'd finished. Was it just her addled mind that had her voice coming out faint and husky?

He patted her dry, then said, "No problem."

"I, uh, suppose I should get back upstairs to clean that mess."

"I'll do it," he said. "You're due at the Oak Valley Center in thirty minutes, and before you go, you should get something to eat."

She'd been so caught up in the study of fascinating dark gold swirls in his eyes, she'd almost forgotten about her once-a-week visit to one of the franchise daycares in a neighboring town. "I appreciate the offer," she said, "but what kind of example would I be setting for the children? You know, when I'm all the time harping about cleaning up your own messes."

"Last I saw," he said, nodding toward the still-snoozing kids, "no one witnessed the incident but me, and…" Grinning, making the universal sign of a key locking his lips, he said, "I'll never tell."

"Anyone ever tell you you're a sweet-potato pie, Travis Callahan?"

He flashed her a grin so handsome that for a full three seconds she forgot to breathe. "Hey, I agreed to keep your secret, so do me a favor and keep mine."

Chapter Nine

At eight that night, after Beulah had left from another
not entirely unpleasant visit—especially seeing how
she'd brought more pickles and a homemade carrot
cake—Travis had just shut down his computer, then
rammed a frozen lasagna in the oven when a knock
sounded on the front door.

Libby sat in her high chair awaiting her dinner—
not very patiently, judging by the fitful cries coming
from her pouty lips.

"Hold your horses," he said, closing the oven
before heading for the front door. "Be with you in
just a sec."

Not that he'd become an expert or anything, but
he was almost getting the hang of the whole domes-
ticity thing, although it would be considerably easier
once the new appliances he'd ordered came in.

Thank god the local Sears—a catalogue-only affair—seemed to have never heard of Beulah, meaning
they'd been all too happy to accept his check for the

new appliances the store had promised to deliver and install by the end of next week.

Kit and his other coworkers—not to mention his friends and business associates he kept in touch with back home—had pointed out that he was spending an awful lot of money on the old place, seeing how he'd only be around until after the judge declared the will rock-solid. But the way he saw it, the old place needed sprucing up. Since there wasn't anything better to do—other than dwell on Kit's pending nuptials—it was at least a mentally healthy way to pass time. Not only that—what better tribute to his sister than to finish the restoration job she'd so lovingly started?

"Hi," Kit said when he opened the door. She'd changed from her navy work slacks and yellow blouse into hip-hugging jeans and a sleeveless halter that showed way more skin than state regulations should allow when it came to preschool-teacher apparel. In her hands she held a foil-covered glass casserole dish.

Waaaaaagggggggghhhhh!

"If this is a bad time," she said, "I'll be happy to—"

"Come on in," he said, giving himself a mental thump for being so ridiculously happy to see her— and not just because what she carried smelled warm and cheesy. Whenever he was around her, he felt almost normal again. Like his old self—whoever that was. "I was just putting dinner in the oven, but what you have smells better."

"If you already have a meal planned," she said, "you can freeze this for another time."

Waaaaaaaaaaaa!

"No way," he said, already heading toward the kitchen. "Come on in. In case you couldn't tell, the princess is throwing a bit of a fit."

"Anything I can help with?"

"You know girls…" He cast a grin over his shoulder. "Probably boy trouble."

"No doubt." She set her dish on the empty counter. In anticipation of the kitchen contractors, the whole kitchen was pretty bare. "What's going on in here?"

He told her about his latest plans for the place and how before the new appliances arrived a lot of other items such as floors, countertops and cabinets needed to be replaced.

"During construction, what're you going to do about food?" she asked, unlatching Libby's seat belt to tug her out of the high chair and into her arms. The infant calmed. Still huffy and puffy but more interested in Kit's kissing and cooing and dangling gold earrings than Travis's dinner—or lack thereof.

"You look good like that," he said, blurting the first thing that'd come to mind.

"Like what?" she asked, genuine confusion in her green eyes.

"Having my baby in your arms."

"Gee, thanks," she said, not sounding all that pleased.

"Sorry." After conking his forehead, he said, "That came out wrong. What I meant was, I've never seen a woman look more at peace holding a child. Well, unless we're talking about Marlene, but—"

"That's okay," she said, touching his shoulder just enough to make him crave more. Hell, not just her touch. Her companionship. Her laughter. "I get it. And I'm sorry for being so touchy." She removed her earring before Libby removed her ear. While he accepted her apology, Travis couldn't help but wonder what else lurked behind her suddenly wounded expression.

"You all right?" he asked.

"Yeah." She nodded, but her throat convulsed as if maybe she was swallowing back tears.

"Hey," he said, surprising himself with the amount of emotion in his own voice. The last thing he wanted was for her to be sad. "What's up?"

"Nothing." After a strangled laugh, she shook her head. "Who am I trying to kid? Everything. I came over here to apologize for being so testy all day, it's just that Levi and I—"

"You broke up?" Travis asked, surprised again by how much he hoped his assumption was true. Kit deserved better than a hardware store owner. She deserved Paris and Rome and being draped in diamonds, rubies and pearls. Not that he was in any way suggesting he be the one to do all that—just that that's the kind of guy she deserved. "Is he cheating on you? If so, I'll—"

He fisted his right hand, slamming it into the palm of his left.

"No," she said, easing her hands around his, dissipating his anger with just one simple touch. "You've got it all wrong. Levi's as wonderful as ever. He just…" She regretfully released Travis to turn toward the counter, using her free hand to remove the foil covering her casserole.

"What?"

She shook her head, then helped herself to the freezer, fishing out a pack of frozen peas. "This is going to sound silly, but I think he loves the rest of this town more than me."

"Huh?" Nose wrinkled and eyebrows scrunched, he said, "That doesn't even make sense."

"Hear me out and you'll see it does." She grabbed a saucepan from the pile of pans and dishes he'd mounded on the table. "Levi has this constant need to help anyone and everyone who stumbles by, usually when we're on a date. It's never really bothered me before, but lately… Last week, as we were leaving for a movie, it was Luigi Fischer, who'd blown three fuses in his new trailer. The week before that, George Wayan had an overflowing toilet while we were having dinner. This week, his neighbor Jim's lawn mower blade needed sharpening. So, see? The man seems to care about everyone and everything way more than me. Sometimes I get the feeling he doesn't really want to marry me and regrets asking me." By now, she was crying quietly.

Travis went to her, awkwardly putting his arms around her and his niece.

"That's not even the worst part," she said. "Sometimes I even catch myself wondering if he's the right man for me. Or if I've been forcing the marriage issue because of how much I feel ready to finally start a family or because of my rule to date only locals. Chrissy says my rule's nuts. But because of what happened with you—then again with Brad Foley—I really feel it's the best way to go."

"Wow," Travis said once she'd managed to somewhat calm down. "You have had a lot to think about. Care to expound on…what was his name? Brad? Do I need to beat him up?"

"Stop fooling around. I'm serious."

"Think I'm not?" he asked.

She pulled back, and though her eyes were red and her complexion wet and blotchy with still-drying tears, never had he seen her more beautiful.

Not that he thought sad looked good on her, just that in her vulnerability she'd shown a side of herself he'd never before seen. Plus, it touched him that of all her friends, he was the one she'd come to for romance advice. Which was why, instead of feeding Libby and putting her bed, then putting Kit in that big old antique tub filled with bubbles, he cleared his throat.

Because in his imagination, the part that came after bubbles had become rather X-rated. As much as he'd tried being impartial, he couldn't help but hope her and Levi's relationship bit the big one so that those full lips of hers would be fair game.

"For three years," she said, "I've been waiting for Levi to take whatever it is we share to the next level."

Travis gulped. "Which would be…?"

"What do you think?" she said through pending tears, making her green eyes shimmer. "Not just promising each other to one day get married but actually doing it."

Travis looked away sharply. The last thing he wanted was for Levi and Kit to actually do the deed. Why then didn't *he* make a play for her now? She'd more or less admitted to trouble in paradise, and all he had to do was side with her. But Levi was a good guy. He'd helped him when he'd needed it. It wasn't cool to dump on your fellow man—especially not over a woman.

So where did that leave Travis?

Basically nowhere. He'd hurt Kit once before and he'd be damned if he did it again.

But what if this time he got it right? He swallowed hard. The past was in the past, and for Kit's own good, he needed to keep it there. He hadn't been right for her then, so what made him think he would be now?

"QUIT HORSING AROUND," Kit scolded after dinner, kneeling alongside Travis beside the claw-foot tub, her blouse wetter than the last time she'd washed it. Libby was all smiles as she sat like a princess on her pink plastic tub throne, squealing with delight each time her new daddy squeaked and splashed her neon-pink rubber duck. "At this rate, we're getting the bathroom cleaner than the baby."

"Lighten up," he said with a grinning nudge. "The place could probably use a good hosing. Just like you could use a good squeaking." He honked the dripping duck in her face, soaking her all the more, then kissing her with it.

When she couldn't help but laugh, he handed the duck to Libby and with free hands traced the creases of Kit's smile. "Much better. That gorgeous grin of yours should be a permanent feature."

When I'm around you, it usually is.

She frowned at the outrageous thought.

"Now what's wrong?" he asked.

"Nothing." She poured a dollop of no-tears shampoo into her palm, then started washing Libby's hair. The simple task combined with Travis's heady presence nearly brought her to tears. No wonder Marlene had been so happy with her lot in life. Great man, great baby, great job. What more did a woman need?

Before Travis's arrival, Kit had been content to mosey along status quo. But losing Marlene and, in a sense, gaining Travis had brought on a discontentedness the likes of which physically hurt. What was it about her life she no longer found good enough?

"This mood of yours wouldn't still be about Levi, would it? Why hasn't the guy found the balls to set a wedding date?"

His bluntness made her wince, but she could hardly correct Travis when he spoke the truth.

"You're right," she said, rinsing Libby's hair, loving the feel of warm, soapy water and soft baby hair all the more when Travis leaned closer to help. Being enveloped in his manly scent and Libby's sweet, simple goodness made her long to experience this sort of uncomplicated domestic bliss every night even more. "I'm ready to get married—now." *Only maybe not to the man I'm engaged to.*

"Tell him."

Tell Levi what? That after all my nagging about setting a wedding date, I'm debating about calling off the engagement? That I find myself shamefully wanting to explore a reunion with you? That all those years ago, when you broke things off with me, I'd wished I'd been mature enough to fight harder to hold on?

Dizzy with the force of her seesawing emotions, she shook her head. No. This was madness, thinking what she and Travis once shared could ever be recaptured. Their summer had been akin to fireflies caught in a jar. At summer's end, their light had gone out. He was leaving IdaBelle Falls as soon as he could, and she couldn't risk getting hurt like that again.

"Trust me," he softly said, reaching for her hand, easing his fingers between hers beneath the water's deliciously warm cover. "Levi doesn't have a clue how you're feeling. But if he did, I'm sure he'd be just as eager to set a wedding date as you."

Why was it then fate chose to twinkle the bathroom's overhead light off her pear-shaped diamond engagement ring?

Never had Kit missed Marlene more. What was fate trying to tell her? That she'd be doing the right thing in prodding Levi to finally set a wedding date? That forcing him into a marriage he wasn't ready for was the wrong thing? Or was she reading too much into every little thing and the only reminder was to next time remove her good jewelry before splashing in the tub?

"YOU'LL NEVER GUESS WHO that was," Beulah said Monday morning, hanging up the kitchen phone.

Frank sat at the table, reading the paper. Thankful for what had thus far been a perfectly peaceful morning.

Before taking the call, his wife had been whipping up a batch of her world-famous strawberry waffles. He'd always loved them, as did Libby when they were broken into bite-size pieces with plenty of syrup and whipped cream.

"All right," his wife said. "Since you're apparently all out of guesses, I'll tell you. That was Clarissa Stevens on the phone."

"Oh?" His reading glasses dangerously close to avalanching off the end of his nose, he pushed them back up, then snapped the paper to the next page.

"And can you guess what she said?"

"Nope, I'm fairly certain I can't."

"I'll help." She abandoned her waffles in favor of her most beloved pastime—gossip. Pulling out the chair opposite Frank's, she had a seat, then took a deep breath. "Well, you know Marlene's friend Kit, right?"

"Yes'm."

"Well, I have it on good authority that last night—" She got up to bustle around the table, whispering the last part in Frank's ear.

"What's with the mystery?" he asked. "No one's around to hear us but the waffle iron. Last I heard, unlike you, she wasn't one to talk."

"The mystery is," Beulah said with a grunt, hands on her hips, chest all puffed up like an indignant turkey's, "while I have the news on good authority, it still could be rumor. And you know darned well I never was one for spreading gossip. The fact is this just won't do."

"Mind telling me why ever not?"

Harrumph. "Don't you know anything?"

Nose back in his paper, he muttered, "Apparently not."

"COFFEE?" TRAVIS ASKED Monday morning, holding out a steaming mug.

Kit glanced up from the happy trance she'd been in all morning but had been trying to hide until Chrissy and Stephanie had the kids occupied with crafts. "No, thanks," she said with a bubble of laughter. "I'm high enough. Caffeine would literally send me flying over the moon."

"I hear it's chilly up there this time of year." He grinned. But whereas that devilish smile of his usually sent her pulse racing, on this most special of mornings only one man held that power. "Be sure to pack a sweater."

"Ha-ha." She was so excited to share her news she actually fidgeted in her kitchen chair. "Travis, you're not going to believe this, but your advice worked."

"What advice?" he asked, stirring cream and no less than eight spoonfuls of sugar into his coffee. Did he usually use that much?

"You know. About Levi. Remember how after dinner Thursday night, while we gave Libby her bath, you said I should talk to him? Really tell him how I've been feeling?" Only, what Travis hadn't known was that she hadn't even been sure what she'd been feeling. And that Kit had just about convinced herself that her problem was Travis. Wanting him. *But if that were true, how could I now be at peace over at least having reached a decision?*

"I said all that?" he asked, adding so much sugar his mug overflowed.

"Here," she said, hopping up from the table to help clean the spill. "You really should pay more attention to what you're doing."

"I was."

"Uh-huh," she said with a teasing frown.

"Well?" He sipped at his concoction, blanched, then poured it down the stainless-steel sink's drain. "What's your news?"

"Can you believe it? Levi did it! Actually committed to a wedding date. Eek!"

"How fantastic!" Chrissy said, abandoning her charges to come running. "I couldn't help but overhear, what with you eeking and all." Seizing Kit's left hand, she said, "Let me rub the engagement ring in case I should ever be so lucky."

"Congratulations," Stephanie gushed, fawning over Kit's ring that Kit had spent a good portion of the morning polishing till it shone like new. She'd told herself she'd wanted a clean ring to signify this fresh start with her fiancé. But had it truly been more of an attempt to snuff her blossoming affection for Travis? "You're so lucky. Levi's a great guy."

Yes, Levi was a great guy. So what'd made their relationship feel tarnished?

She looked up to catch Travis staring.

At which point she told herself the chills rippling through her had more to do with the overzealous AC unit than any connection with him.

"I wanna see your ring, Miss Kit!" Four-year-old Bonnie Vitucci dashed over.

As did every one of her fifteen classmates. Before Kit knew it, they were hosting an impromptu cookies-and-milk party in her honor.

"Way to go," Travis said once the hullabaloo had settled down and the kids had returned to making picnic baskets from mini milk cartons. "If this is truly what you want, I'm happy for you."

"Why wouldn't it be what I want?" she asked, bristling, swiping harder than necessary at the already crumb-free counter.

"Did I imply it wasn't?" His voice hit her as being unexpectedly tender. Stopping her midswipe, he took her hands in his and squeezed, creating a knot in her throat. Why did his approval of her engagement mean so much? "As my sister's best friend, I care what happens to you. I want you to have a great life, Kit. You deserve it."

All choked up, she snatched her hands free and tossed her arms around him in a big hug. "Has anyone ever told you that when you're not grumbling about your current living conditions you're off-the-charts adorable?"

"When have I ever grumbled?"

"Let's see," she said, pulling back to tap her index finger to her smiling lips. "First—"

He rolled his eyes. "Don't you have better things to do than harass me? Like plan a wedding?"

Yes, as a matter of fact, she did have wedding plans to attend to. But first she'd launch a full-scale self-examination as to why Travis's approval of her upcoming nuptials held all the fun of a popped balloon.

Chapter Ten

"Tell me," Travis said that night to his niece, currently cooing at a duck decal on her changing table, "in all that flapping about wedding plans, did Kit ever once mention loving the guy?"

Aaaaeeeeayya.

"Thank you. I thought you'd agree." Now a diaper expert, he whipped off her dirty one, wiped her bottom, puffed on powder, then had her in a fresh diaper in record time. Snapping the buttons closed on her yellow jumper, he said, "You ask me, I think she's more in love with the notion of getting married than being married. I mean, if she thinks it's a drag hanging with Mr. Fix-It now, what's she think it's going to be like in twenty years?"

Eeeergurglaya.

"See? I knew you were wise beyond your years." Scooping her from the changing table and into his arms, he added, "You would never marry a guy just to pick out fancy flowers and a dress, would you?"

She ignored him in favor of lunging for the over-all-wearing goose on her crib's mobile.

"Women," he said with a shake of his head.

After he kissed and tucked in Libby for the night, Travis headed to his room.

What he was supposed to do once he got there, he didn't know. He'd meant to order a TV for the bedroom but had been so busy working on the kitchen he'd forgotten. Guess he could read—there were plenty of financial reports to catch up on—but that sounded like a snooze.

Seeing how it was too early to go to bed and he wasn't the least bit tired, he wandered downstairs and out onto the front porch.

The three dogs trailed after him.

Somewhere across town—thankfully not in his backyard—a train wailed.

Marlene and Gary had hung a rickety old swing from the porch's pale blue ceiling, so Travis helped himself to a seat, hauling Cocoa up beside him.

The night was beautiful. Hot and muggy, but the sweet scent of grass he'd mowed filled him with pride. He swatted at a whiny mosquito, but his enjoyment of the sound of chirping crickets overrode the momentary annoyance. So far from true civilization, out here stars shone differently—more brilliant—than they did in Chicago. It was like a whole new sky he never tired of viewing.

Rubbing Cocoa's silky ears, he wondered how

many times Marlene and Gary had sat out here doing nothing but sharing their days and gazing at the stars.

He'd have liked that, being able to share the view with someone special. But seeing how his only true friend in town was Kit and she was spoken for—thanks in large part to his big mouth—he couldn't count on her for companionship.

There was Chrissy, who seemed genuinely nice and caring.

And that new girl—what was her name? She'd made it clear she could be into him given the slightest coaxing. Question was, why wasn't he into her?

Right now he couldn't seem to think of any woman but his sister and how much he missed her. He regretted not being more supportive of the way she'd chosen to live her life. And when his mind drifted from thoughts of Marlene, there was Kit to contend with and his confusion over what might've been.

To this day, they had chemistry.

She might be marrying another man, but she sure as hell felt good in Travis's arms. Soft. Inviting.

If he closed his eyes and tilted his head just right, he could remember their brief kiss. The way her lips fit against his, the way he'd been on the verge of going further when she'd put the kibosh on his fun.

Hot damn, kissing her had been fun.

Was Lucky Levi tasting her right now? Running his hands up her back, tracing the gentle swell of her waist to her hips? Maybe pinching a bit of her sweet behind?

The mere thought of what Levi had and he didn't got Travis to his feet.

Cocoa whined at the disruption in her nap when the swing rocked.

"Get over it," Travis said when all three dogs shot him dirty looks for corralling them back inside. "And would one of you please tell me where to find the antacid?"

"LEVI, HONEY," KIT SAID in his garage Monday night, "please stop tinkering and talk to me. We have a lot to do and not a lot of time."

From beneath his truck he said, "Can't you just handle it, sweetie? Then I'll be surprised when I show up for our vows."

Peering under the vehicle, she tried not to breathe too deeply of the dirty-sock stench of old motor oil. "Don't you want to plan our wedding together? It'll be romantic. You know, making sure everything's just right for the first day of the rest of our lives."

He slid out from under the front bumper. "Huh?"

"Think about it. Our wedding day launches our lives."

"Aren't we kind of already alive? And, hell, seeing how I practically live at your place, I don't see how all that much is going to change."

"Actually…" she said, licking her lips, then taking a deep breath. "Funny you mentioned that—you hanging so much at my place—because I was just thinking that to make our wedding night extra special we should live apart until the ceremony."

He got a stricken look. "And not…?"

"Would it kill you to be abstinent till the end of August?"

"Yes," he said without hesitation.

"All right…" Arms crossed, lips pressed into a frown, she said, "I'll plan the entire ceremony on my own, but I feel very strongly that we should be apart until our wedding day."

"I feel more strongly we shouldn't be apart."

"Levi…" Was it wrong of her to ask this?

He groaned. "Do you want to marry me or just have the perfect wedding and wedding night?"

"That's mean—and totally out of left field. Of course I want to marry you."

"Just not sleep with me?"

It was a loaded question. Why didn't she want to sleep with him until the wedding? If she truly loved him, shouldn't she be dying to be in his arms 24/7?

"Kit?" he prodded.

"Finish your oil change," she said in a huff, already leaving the garage. "I'd prefer talking about this when you're not under a car." Better yet, when she knew the answer herself.

She loved Levi. He was one of her dearest friends. Dearest *friend?*

What was wrong with her that all of a sudden being friends with her future husband didn't seem like enough? She wanted fire and passion and excitement.

In short, she wanted to feel the way she'd once felt with Travis. She knew the magic of their summer could never be recreated, so why couldn't she let it go?

Before he'd blown back into her life, she'd been happy, content. Right? Had she truly been both of those things or merely complacent? Satisfied to settle?

Hands to her throbbing forehead, Kit aimed for her car. Levi was a wonderful man. Kind and caring, and when they were together—which was rare these days—fun. She wouldn't be settling if she married him. She'd be lucky. Everyone she knew agreed— even Marlene, once she'd gotten over the ridiculous notion that she and Travis might once again find each other. So what was the problem?

Damned if Kit knew, but now that the wedding date was set, the clock was ticking on the time she had left to figure it out.

"SO THEN YOU SEE WHY I'm upset?" Kit asked Travis early Thursday evening. Since the day had been relatively cool, as well as hectic, they now indulged in a much-needed break on his front porch swing, Libby cooing between them with each forward rock. Absentmindedly stroking the baby's downy-soft hair, she complained, "I had to pick out our wedding cake all by myself. Don't you think it was Levi's place to have been there?"

"Absolutely."

"That was fast," she said with a sideways glance. "Are you agreeing with me out of the goodness of your heart or because I offered to cook you and Libby dinner, seeing how your kitchen's still a disaster?"

"Absolutely." The handsome grin he flashed her way somersaulted her stomach.

"You're awful."

"Why? Just because I happen to think a cake's a pile of flour and sugar and nothing to get all jacked up about?"

"I'm hardly jacked up," she argued. "Just wanting my fiancé to share in the planning of what's supposed to be the most important day of our lives."

Libby lunged a little too far forward. Kit and Travis caught her in tandem.

Laughing with relief, Kit said, "That was close."

"Nah, we make a good team. The kid was never in a lick of danger."

"Lick of danger, huh?"

"What's wrong? You're eyeing me like I've got a bug on the end of my nose."

"Nothing," she said, scooping Libby onto her lap for safekeeping and kisses. "Just that for a minute there, I caught you sounding like a Southerner."

He rolled his eyes. "Trust me, soon as this custody thing is over, Libby and I are heading for the big city. I talked to my contractor today and her nursery is almost done."

"Great." And it was. It warmed Kit's heart knowing Travis was making Libby her own special nest in his Chicago home. The trouble was not the home but the faraway place.

"If it's so great, what's with the sad face?"

"Is it wrong of me to know I'm going to miss you?"

Grinning, he eased his arm atop her shoulders and said, "Why, Miss Wells, I'm flattered."

"Yeah, well, you shouldn't be." She elbowed him before nuzzling the crown of Libby's head, seeking comfort in this little reminder of how she used to share moments like this with her best friend. And Levi. What did it mean that she now spent more time with Travis than she ever had with her fiancé?

"That's my girl. Always have to get in the last line."

"Yep."

They exchanged smiles, then sat for a few minutes in silence save for chirping crickets and a few wrens bickering in the birdbath.

"So?" Travis asked, fingering one of Libby's curls. "You ever gonna tell me about this amazing cake you were forced to buy all on your lonesome?"

"IT'S OFFICIAL," BEULAH said to Frank that evening on her way through the back door. He sat at the kitchen table working a puzzle of a Holland windmill. It was surrounded by yellow and red tulips she found very appealing—or at least would once he'd finished that section.

"What is?" he asked without looking up.

"Well, since you asked, I was just at the beauty parlor for my standing appointment, when who should walk in but Helen Mitchell—you know, the one who does wedding cakes."

"Uh-huh."

"Well, she said that just this afternoon Kit was at her place picking out a cake."

"She still marrying that hardware store boy? What's his name? Levi something—like the jeans."

"Levi Petty," she said with a snort, setting her oversize white leather purse on the kitchen counter so her hands would be free to fix herself an iced tea. "And his momma named him that because that's what she was wearing when he was born."

"Ask me," Frank said, "seems awfully tough for a woman to give birth wearin' blue jeans."

"I'm just relaying what I heard, seeing how I'm not one to talk. Anyway, the boy's taken years to set a wedding date. Why now? Right when everything was going along so well?"

With a grunt Frank asked, "Thought everything was bad? You know, what with you being caught up in a big court case and all?"

She eyed him for a long minute, then turned on her heel, heading straight for the always-stocked cookie jar. "Haven't you ever heard sometimes bad is good?"

"BUT, LEVI," KIT SAID into her kitchen's cordless phone that night while adding butter to mashed potatoes, "Travis and Libby are here, and I even made a ham."

"Sounds fantastic," Levi said, "but Carol Kline's son's ferret got stuck in a sewage drainage pipe, and it's gnawed its way out. Did a crapload—pardon the pun—of damage to some plastic piping, as well. Neil West—remember meeting him? My plumbing bud? Well, he's out here with me, and we're trying to get her hooked back up by dark."

"Okay," Kit said, trying to sound understanding even though she was tired of being the absolute last item on her fiancé's priority list. "Just get here as soon as you can, okay?"

"You know I will." He blew her a kiss, then disconnected.

Kit put the phone back on the charger, then added more butter to the potatoes. At the rate she was going, her groom wouldn't even be at the wedding to see her in her dress, so why worry about her figure when at the moment she needed comfort—now.

Usually, puttering in her cheerful yellow-and-white kitchen with the worn brick floor and her Blue Willow china collection was one of her favorite things to do. At the moment, though, she felt more like throwing herself across her bed, indulging in a nice, long cry.

"Everything all right?" Travis asked from his seat at the kitchen table, jiggling a grinning Libby on his knee.

"Yes," she lied.

"Then what's with the frown?" Bouncing Libby, making her giggle, he said in a high falsetto, "Smile, Aunt Kit!"

Kit managed a half grin.

"Come on," Travis said, rising with Libby and repositioning her to sit on his shoulders. "You can do better than that."

"Outlook doubtful." Kit checked the ham and added glaze. "Now," she said to Libby, turning around to reach up and grab her chubby hand, "if I had a big stud hauling me around on his shoulders, then I'd be all smiley like you."

Chuckling, Travis said, "Seems to me a certain girl around here named Kit used to *ride* me all the time."

"What?" Kit blurted, face surely as red as the cherries she'd put in the center of the ham's pineapple rings! The size of his wicked grin told her he knew exactly how his seemingly innocent statement had sounded. The beast!

"Don't tell me you don't remember all those games of chicken we used to play with Marlene down in the old fishing hole. My shoulders ached from having your big butt lounging around on me all day."

"I don't have a big butt," she protested, swatting his chest.

"Watch it," he said. "I'm holding a baby. And for the record, no. You don't have a big butt now and you didn't have one then, but hey—" he winked "—you gotta admit it got you going."

That earned him another swat.

Kit's grown-up dinner companion plunked Libby into the high chair Kit had picked up at a yard sale for the baby she was growing perilously close to, then helped get their meal to the table. A part of Kit wanted to kick her table decor up a notch—maybe add a few candles and flowers—but figured without Levi there, it probably wouldn't be appropriate. So in the end she fixed a nibbler platter of peas and applesauce and potatoes and minced cherries and pineapples for Libby, then sat down with the charmer's uncle at her plain-Jane table, determined to have a good time yet fearing that with Travis, she couldn't have anything *but* fun.

"THAT WAS PHENOMENAL," Travis said, clearing the table for Kit while she took it easy after having cooked such a feast. "Thank you."

"You're welcome."

After he'd washed a few dishes and she'd gotten antsy and hopped up to put the leftovers in storage containers and Libby had fallen asleep on a blanket on the living room carpet, Kit asked, "Do you think it's always going to be like this?"

"What do you mean?" He put a dried glass in the cabinet to the left of the sink.

"With Levi. Do you think I'm setting myself up for a lifetime of lonely nights?"

"Thanks a lot," he said. "Good to know I'm such a bore."

"You know what I mean." She smacked his butt with the Saran wrap.

Funny how the woman was always touching him or swatting him or hugging him as she had this afternoon. He liked it but shouldn't. While his brain understood her being promised to another guy, his body was clueless. He wanted her—bad. Not a good thing.

"Levi was supposed to be here but then at the last

minute bailed. I know he likes helping people and it's part of his job, but what about spending time with me? We're supposed to be planning our wedding, but he always manages to avoid it."

"He's spending time with their plumbing, Kit. Plumbing. There's a difference between him helping folks and abandoning you."

"I know," she said, walking toward him so he couldn't help but pull her into his arms, resting his cheek on her soft hair, breathing in her honeysuckle smell. "But that doesn't make me miss him any less. I've told him this, but he thinks I'm just stressed because of the wedding."

"Are you missing him?" Travis asked. "Or that ideal family picture you've had rattling around in your head?"

"What's that supposed to mean?" She pulled back. "You implying I don't love him?"

Hands in his pockets, leaning against the counter, he gave her a disinterested shrug.

"Because I do. He's a great guy. Everyone in town thinks so."

"Myself included. Hell, I'd've died if he hadn't put in those AC units for me."

"See?" she said. "He's wonderful like that. So why do I have this constant craving for *more?*"

"Because he happens to suck in the romance department?"

"Did I say that?"

No, but she was sure as hell implying it by

bringing up the subject—especially with him. She had plenty of girlfriends to hash all of this over with, so why was she choosing to spill such intimate details to him? Could it be her fiancé angst had less to do with Levi and everything to do with the truth that had been staring them in the face from the moment she'd shown up in his office? The truth that they didn't just share chemistry but a fierce attraction as undeniable as it was wrong.

But if Kit broke up her engagement?

His heart beat faster just thinking of the delicious possibility. He knew he was wrong for her, but like Beulah's high cholesterol feasts, when it came to spending time with Kit, touching her, kissing her, he couldn't stop wanting more.

Travis asked, "When's the last time you made love?"

"What's it any of your business?"

"That long, huh?"

"Yes, but because that's how I want it. That way, on our wedding night it'll be more—"

"Hot?" Travis asked, snagging her around her waist not because it was the right thing to do but because, plain and simple, he wanted her back in his arms. "The way it used to be between us, Kit? Remember when we opened that Pandora's box with that first raw kiss? There was no closing it after that. I remember wanting you so damned bad I'd lay awake in my bedroom, counting the ways I'd like to kiss you. Clothes on, off, didn't make much difference—who am I trying to kid?" he said with a chuckle. "Hell, yeah, it mattered, but the end result was always the same. Our chemistry was way off the charts. I wanted you to be my girl."

"Then why'd you leave me?" she asked quietly, her words warm and husky against his chest. What would it be like to feel her against him like this, only him with no shirt? And her with no shirt and—

Inching back, he cupped his hands to her cheeks, raising her face to his, locking her gaze to his.

"I'm going to kiss you," he said.

She shook her head, then faintly nodded.

And if she hadn't? Would he have had the strength, the character to pull back? Didn't much matter seeing how she'd given her consent. The trip to her lips seemed endless. Like a journey he'd waited a lifetime to complete. When he was almost there, at the end of the road that'd finally bring him home, she parted her lips, releasing a faint, breathy mew, which only made him want her more.

He was hard. So damned hard.

While he knew he had no right asking for even a single kiss, let alone more, that didn't stop the wanting. The aching for forbidden fruit.

Kiss me...her wistful expression urged.

And he almost did—until the front door slammed open.

Waaaaaagggghuh!

"Sorry, Libby," Levi said, his voice muffled. "Didn't mean to give you a scare."

Kit backed away hastily, tidied her hair.

Travis let her go.

"Kit, honey!" Levi called, Libby in his arms as he entered the cozy kitchen that would one day soon be his home—not Travis's. "Hey, you two. Have fun?"

Chapter Eleven

"What did you do?"

"Huh?" Travis took one look at Kit and scratched his head. Wasn't it obvious? Marlene's former drab living room was now a state-of-the-art business center, complete with a hard-edged chrome-and-glass desk and plenty of high-tech equipment to fill it. "Don't you like it? Once I found out the FedEx man wasn't under Beulah's evil clutches, I ordered all of this. Check out the computer," he said, hustling behind his desk. "Latest thing on the market. Can't even buy it in stores yet."

"Wonderful," Kit said, her arms crossed, lips pressed into a frown. "So I'm assuming this is why you called in sick this morning?"

"Steph said she had everything handled."

"But I needed you."

"That mean you're finally admitting how bad you want me?" He looked up from his jumbo flat-screen monitor and grinned.

"You know how I meant it, Mr. Smart-A—"

"Hey, watch it, there's a kid present." He gestured over his shoulder to Libby, who was on her back snoozing in a new bassinet.

"Sorry," she said, casting a glance toward Libby, then shaking her head.

"What's your problem?" he asked. "I thought you'd be as excited as I am about me regaining some semblance of normalcy."

"My problem is that Marlene would've hated this. Gary, too. They had big plans for this room—none of which included turning their formal front parlor into a shrine to commerce. And for that matter, why are you spending so much money on the place when you're leaving just as soon as the judge grants you custody?"

"Last we spoke, my lawyer said everything's set for our day in court. As for my money, I thought it was mine to spend. You don't like what I'm doing with the place, Kit, feel free to find the door."

"So that's how it's going to be? What was I supposed to do last night, Travis?"

"Leave him."

"What?" She froze.

"Yes, I hurt you in the past, but I'm sorry. So damned sorry. Who knows? Maybe we're all wrong for each other, but if it's so wrong, why, Kit, does every time we touch feel right?"

"I'm engaged," she stressed. "Levi's going to be my husband."

"That's all well and good, but do you love him?

'Cause seems to me," he said, walking toward her, "if you loved him, you wouldn't want to be anywhere near me. Yet here you are."

"You're an ass," she said, terrified of the implications of his deeply cutting words.

Why didn't Travis understand that no matter how much she craved his kisses or, God forbid, going further, she couldn't? She wasn't marrying Levi on a lark. She loved him. He was good and stable, and okay, so things might've been rocky as of late, but he wasn't the type to one day stop returning her calls. He was loyal. Travis might've apologized for the way he'd behaved all those years ago, but those were just words. She had yet to see just how much he'd actually changed. Granted, he'd been wonderful with Libby, but what did that prove about where he stood on marriage? Lifelong commitment?

As much as she was attracted to Travis, he scared her, as well. She was terrified of the restless yearning just being around him evoked within her. With Levi, Kit felt safe and secure. With Travis, it was as if she was consumed by a never-satisfied itch. Which was why she would ignore his suggestion to leave a man who'd done nothing wrong.

Except not to be Travis.

"And that's why you love me." As if trying his damnedest to lighten the suddenly heavy mood, he added with a broad smile, "At least I hope you love me."

She shook her head. "Anyone ever told you, you're nuts?"

"No one but you would dare."

"And Beulah," she taunted.

"You just had to bring her up." Taking Kit by her hand for the sole reason of torturing himself, he led her to the kitchen. "Come on. Hopefully you'll forgive my office once you see this."

"Whoa," Kit said when they walked into the kitchen. She told herself to release Travis's hand but wasn't strong enough to follow through and actually let go. "It's beautiful."

"Told you." Though he grinned, she spied the slightest bit of hurt in his eyes. As if he were a little boy excited about showing off a toy and she'd told him it was ugly. Which his office was, placed like some alien spaceship's cockpit smack-dab in the middle of a lovely antebellum home. But the kitchen…

Kit held tight to his hand, but only because if she didn't, the room's unexpected wonder would bring her to tears. Marlene had desperately wanted the space redone.

Tall cherry cabinets lined yellow pin-striped walls. A new fridge had been ingeniously covered in wood that matched the cabinets, making it blend in. The countertops were white marble. The floors, softly glowing walnut. There was even a small black wrought-iron table set with yellow calico cushions lining each seat in the coved breakfast nook. A huge bouquet of yellow daisies graced the glass-topped table's center.

"How…?" she managed to mumble.

"With enough cash in the right hands," he said, "you'd be amazed at the possibilities."

As much as Kit knew that, per Marlene's dying wishes, she should lecture Travis on thinking money could solve everything, this was one case where it apparently had. Libby even had a new high chair. Gorgeous antique-looking cherry with a floral yellow laminated cushion that could be wiped clean easily.

"Look at this," he said, proudly tugging her to another feature of the room.

Now she did cry.

Instantly.

Painfully.

And as usual, Travis was right there to hold her.

Hanging on the backside of the den's brick fireplace was an exquisite oil painting of Marlene and Gary, seated on a blue gingham blanket beneath a rambling oak. Surrounded by a field of blue and white wildflowers, Gary wore a white suit, Marlene a flowing white dress. The artist was a master of light, immersing the couple in a playground of dappled sun.

"How…?" Again Kit wondered how Travis had managed to pull this off but couldn't find words to ask.

"I have a friend of a friend back in Chicago who knows the artist," he said. "When I mentioned wanting something special, he hooked me up. I sent the artist their wedding pictures, and voilà."

"It's amazing," Kit said. "Libby will be so glad to have it."

"Yeah…" Travis sounded choked up himself.

"Seeing this painting, I retract my earlier statement."

"About me being an ass?"

Still misty-eyed, she nodded.

"But no formal apology?"

Holding his hand tightly, she smacked his chest with her free one. "You'd better not push your luck."

"I WAS PLANNING ON something simple…" Saturday afternoon Kit eyed a particularly beautiful page of the floral catalogue IdaBelle Falls' only florist had given her. She and Chrissy sat at a catalogue-covered table in the store's all-white wedding planning section. Being in the shop, smelling the rich mingling of flower scents, was akin to being seated in a little slice of heaven. Roses and carnations and lilies all vied for attention—with the store's occupants ultimately winning by sampling the heady blend. "Daisies maybe. But these orchids are amazing. You can order them?"

"Technically," said Dixie Zayborn, a towering gorgeous forty-something blonde who referred to herself as *"Z" Most Fabulous Floral Designer,* "I can get any flower, grown in any region of the world—just know it's going to be expensive if it's not in season."

"Sure…" Kit gazed at the array of orchid photos Dixie had shown her. To Chrissy she said, "How amazing would it be with my ivory cake to have ivory orchids? Everywhere. These." She tapped a photo of a creamy bloom with a violet streak running down the center. "These are what I want. My brides-maids' dresses can be dyed purple to match. And I'll have ivy and ferns with the flowers—not standard ferns, but one of those delicate mini varieties."

"Of course," Dixie said. "But for these particular orchids, per stem we're talking at least fifteen bucks, plus overnight-air fees. Also, they're so delicate it'll take forever to arrange them without bruising."

Kit nibbled her lower lip.

She *really* wanted orchids.

They smelled so good. And were unexpected. On the other hand, carnations smelled good, too, and were probably dirt cheap. Still, she really wanted orchids and had already saved a boatload on her cake, which must've been why she blurted, "How long will it take to get a cost estimate? Mind you, using just a few orchids as accents. I'd want one or two sprinkled in my bouquet, plus some for the three bridesmaids and one for my flower girl. Then there's the altar décor—the ceremony's being held at King's Chapel—but we'll be frugal there. Oh, and we'll also need arrange-ments for the reception—but nothing fancy."

Writing furiously, Dixie asked, "Where's the re-ception to be, dear?"

"I thought the old stone mill beside the falls might be pretty."

"Pretty, yes, but you have to bring everything in—everything—down to the very last table and chair, which adds a tremendous amount of cost. Have you checked into table rental? There's a store in Harrison.

They also rent china, cutlery and linens. I've worked with them before and will be happy to coordinate, but again, they don't come cheap."

"So, um…" Kit was literally afraid to ask, "How long will it take you to work up an estimate?"

"A few minutes," Dixie said with a smile and a re-assuring pat to her hand. "You two sit tight while I call my supplier."

Once she'd left, Chrissy said, "This is going to be gorgeous."

Nibbling her lower lip, Kit said, "I hope that estimate doesn't come back too high."

"Maybe it won't."

"Yeah." She shot her friend a quick grimace. "Thanks for coming with me. All this is way more fun with a friend."

"You're welcome," Chrissy said with a hug. "I'm glad I came. Gives me practice for when it's my turn."

"Any prospects in mind?" she teased.

"Maybe. Speaking of which…" She wagged her cell. "I forgot I was supposed to call him about dinner tonight. Be right back."

TRAVIS GLANCED at his diner menu. Though he hated dining out alone on a Saturday night, he hoped Kit at least was having fun. Libby, who was at a kid's birthday party with her grandparents, for sure was.

He ordered a BLT and fries, wolfed that down, then sat, eyeing the laughing, talking couples around him. Country music from a jukebox played softly and where ordinarily he couldn't stand the twang, here it felt right.

Before coming to IdaBelle Falls, he didn't used to feel lonely like this. Wistful. Oh sure, he'd gotten the occasional hankering to take off in a big boy toy like that sailboat he'd always planned to buy, but this was different.

What he wanted now wasn't so much a thing but a person. The way he felt when he was with Kit. And Libby. Lately he felt most complete when accompanied by both of them. But he'd said his piece. Tried to broach the subject of Kit breaking her engagement, and obviously, she wasn't interested in even trying to regain what they'd lost—or rather, what he'd given up—which had landed him here.

As long as she was happy, he'd somehow find a way to live within himself. Which was why, when Chrissy had called him that afternoon from the backroom of the florist's shop, asking him if he'd like to join her in getting Kit nicer flowers than she otherwise could've afforded, he'd not only said yes, but volunteered to foot the entire bill. Whatever Kit wanted for her wedding, she could have. Whatever it took to make up for the way he'd hurt her all those years ago.

Snatching his bill from the table, he left a generous tip, then made his way toward the diner's front, where the register sat upon a glass pie case.

Spending the remainder of his god-awful night eating a slice of banana cream pie seemed like just the ticket.

"Why don't you add one of those to my bill," he asked the buxom redhead who'd introduced herself as Olivia Stanford, the establishment's owner.

"I'd be honored," she said, holding bejeweled hands to her rhinestone-covered chest. "And you know, I have to say you're not at all how I'd expected."

"Oh?" he asked, forking over thirty bucks.

"You must know what folks have been saying."

"Uh, no. Care to enlighten me?"

"I really shouldn't," she said, long red nails at her throat. "I don't like to be one to talk."

"Please…"

"Since you pressed…" the restaurateur said, a definite twinkle in her eyes. Reaching beneath the checkout counter, she found a pink-and-blue flyer, then handed it to Travis. "When you first came to IdaBelle Falls, Beulah handed these out to most every business in town."

Travis read the flyer, with its acidic message, barely containing his rage. Who did Beulah think she was? What was the matter with her? Couldn't she see that Libby being raised by him was in her best interest?

And after all, it wasn't as if Chicago was on the other side of the globe; Beulah would be free to visit her granddaughter as often as she liked. He crumpled the flyer like the petty trash it was, but then something occurred to him and he stopped destroying the document to instead flatten it against his chest.

"Thank you," he said, extending his hand to the woman who'd just ensured he won custody of his niece.

"For what?" she asked, shaking his hand, smiling in such a blatant way she told him without a single word she knew exactly what he was thanking her for.

He winked. "For putting the first nail in Beulah Redding's coffin."

Chapter Twelve

"Beulah's coffin?" Kit said once they'd climbed into her car and headed back to Travis's Sunday morning after church. When Levi had called to tell her he couldn't go because one of his employees needed help roofing, she almost stayed home herself. But then Travis had called and mentioned that Beulah would be picking up Libby to take her to her church that morning. Seeing how Travis was already dressed, Kit asked him if he wanted to go with her. "Don't you think that was a little harsh?" she asked after he'd told her about his discovery last night.

Staring out the window at rolling forested hills and bucolic pasture, he shrugged. "I take it you've never heard the saying 'All's fair in love and war'?"

"You honestly feel you're at war with Libby's grandmother?"

"What would you call it?" he asked with a sarcastic laugh. "Libby's legally mine. All Beulah's doing by forcing this custody hearing is delaying the inevitable. I probably shouldn't have let her take Libby this morning."

The reminder that Travis wasn't in IdaBelle Falls by choice but by court edict was something Kit knew she'd needed to hear. Even in the short time he'd been here she'd come to depend on him, his friendship, much as she had his sister. When he and Libby left, it'd be like losing Marlene all over again. Only because she wasn't sure she could go through that kind of pain again, Kit said, "You could stay, you know?"

"W-what?" he all but sputtered. "Why would I want to—"

She locked her gaze on the road.

"Sorry," he said. "I didn't mean that like it sounded."

"No, I'm sorry. Of course you should return to Chicago as soon as possible. That's where your life is."

"You'll be able to visit, you know. Libby, that is. Whenever you'd like. I'll pay for flights for you and Levi to come for weekends. I've been kicking around the notion of buying a boat. Libby and I will take you two out for a sail."

"Sure," she said, swallowing the silly knot in her throat. Why had she even started this? Why did she care whether he left town or not? Yes, on her deathbed Marlene had asked Kit to help Travis see there was more to life than work, but obviously she couldn't accomplish that monumental task in a few weeks. That sort of deprogramming took time. Years. Time with

Travis was one thing she'd never had in the past and would obviously never have in the future.

"What's got you so quiet?" he asked.

"A trip down memory lane."

Leaning his head against the seat rest, he groaned.

"That happy with your past, are you?" She shot him a grin.

"Not that I have all that many regrets, but seeing how limited our contact was in the past and how strained things were left between us—"

"I didn't think they were strained," she said, trying not to sound angry. "They just *weren't*. I mean, one minute you were out of town yet still writing and calling, then the next I never heard from you again."

After turning right onto Yale, she glanced his way to find a muscle ticking in his jaw.

"Not that it matters," he said, "but I didn't want to be—out of your life."

Okay… What was she supposed to do with that revelation?

"Th-then why were you? Why did you just one day act as if you'd never even heard of me?" With the car idling at a stop sign, she angled on her seat to face him. "Do you have any idea what it did to me when I raced home to call you after school, only to have your maid or housekeeper or whoever the hell she was tell me you were no longer accepting my calls?"

Looking down, he took her hands, tenderly brushing the tops with his thumbs. "I'm sorry for that." He met her gaze, squeezing her hands. "Deeply ashamed."

"Then why'd you do it?"

He glanced out the window, then back to her. "Easy answer? Peer pressure."

"And the tough answer?" she prodded.

"Fear." Releasing her, he sighed. "You didn't fit. All my life I'd been told what to do. Shown the so-called right paths. Meeting, let alone falling for a girl from small-town Arkansas was my paternal grandparents' worst nightmare all over again. They'd lived through it with my father and they damn sure weren't going to see me succumb to the so-called dark side, as well."

Lips clamped tight, Kit punched the car's gas pedal. No matter how powerful Travis might seem, he was ultimately a man who did what he was told—even if the only ones still dictating his life's course were ghosts.

"You asked and I told you," he said. "So what's with the cold shoulder?"

She pulled into his driveway and turned off the car. "You're imagining things."

"Come in for a drink."

"I'm busy."

"Am I imagining things?"

Drumming her fingers on the wheel, she said, "It's no secret I have a wedding to plan."

"And…" He fixed her with a stare of such intensity she felt in danger of drowning in it. Grasping for a lifeline that wasn't there. Or was it? Had Travis's admission of why he'd ended things between them signaled a change in their relationship?

"You probably have business of your own to attend to," she said softer than she would've liked.

"At the moment, you and Libby are my business."

"But then you're leaving."

"Does it matter? You'll have Levi to keep you company."

"I know." So then why didn't the thought bring her the comfort it should've?

BACK IN THE DAYCARE ON what should've been an ordinary Monday morning, Travis was leading story hour with a giggling Libby riding on his shoulders. Kit didn't quite know what to think about him anymore. On the one hand, she felt as if they'd become good friends, then came their words after church, leaving her more confused than ever.

A long, long time ago he was much more than a mere friend. But Levi was the great love of her life, right? Levi was the man with whom she'd spend the rest of her days—and nights.

So how come she couldn't quite seem to catch her breath while studying Travis's killer white-toothed smile?

Immersing herself in her work, she jumped when Travis sneaked up behind her at her desk. "Boo!"

"Creep," she reflexively said, spinning her chair to let him have it, only to be faced by the mesmerizing sight of his abs encased in a deceptively casual mossy-green pullover that did amazing tricks to his eyes—once she'd gotten that far in her perusal!

"How could a creep deliver you a present like

this?" From behind his back he pulled a slick black-and-white brochure, handing it to her before settling into Marlene's desk chair.

"I don't mean to be rude, but what is it?" Kit asked. The pamphlet showcased selected works and achievements of Betty Anne Worshire, a world-renowned photographer. "The gift, I mean."

"Isn't it obvious?"

She flipped the pamphlet over, thinking maybe he'd taped a gift certificate for a limited-edition print on the back. "Um, no."

He popped out of his chair to take the brochure from her, then caress it as if he were a *Price Is Right* model. "What we have here, fresh from the mailbox, is but a sampling of the phenomenal works of one of my dearest friends—who, I might add, agreed to move heaven and earth to free up her schedule for your nuptials."

"What?" Kit coughed. "You're kidding, right? B-because Betty Anne takes pics of presidents and Barbra Streisand and…and the Dalai Lama and Richard Gere."

"And now," he said with a charming bow, "she'll be taking pics of you."

"No," she said with a firm shake of her head. "It's too much."

"Please," he teased, parking his big hands on the armrests of her chair. "Let me do this for you. Marlene would approve."

"Levi wouldn't," she said, scrunching her neck

when he playfully nuzzled it, shooting tingly chills of awareness through her the way no other man—even her fiancé—ever could. Losing herself to Travis all over again would be so easy. Trouble was, he wasn't offering anything more than friendship, and she had no right—no desire—to get hurt by him again. Which was why she was marrying Levi. He was stable. Kind, caring, loyal, dependable...

Boring.

Hand to her mouth, throat constricting at the horror of what she'd just thought about the man she was on the verge of spending the rest of her life with, Kit ran from the room.

"HEY," TRAVIS SAID A FEW minutes later, having found her on the back side of the shed. He wrapped his arm around her. "If you'd rather have Fifi's Fancy Fotos do the wedding, I'll completely understand."

"It's not that," she said, laughing, wanting nothing more than to stay next to him forever. Which was ridiculous.

Travis Callahan was like the sky. Limitless, always new and exciting. Also, the sky couldn't be depended upon to stay. Sure, it was there, but not in a tangible way. Like the stars—you couldn't touch them, feel them, count on them to keep you warm on cold winter nights. Which was why she'd vowed years ago to never give a piece of herself to anyone other than a hearty salt-of-the-earth local. Like Levi. Who was a wonderful, wonderful man who wanted to stay in IdaBelle Falls and have a family. Which was why she couldn't for the life of her begin to comprehend what had brought on all these emotions.

Maybe because, despite how wonderful Levi was, he would never be Travis—the man she'd first loved and now judged every other man by.

"I'm in awe that you even thought of hiring a photographer. A-and Levi loves her work. He just bought her new coffee-table book."

"Seriously?"

"Uh-huh." Sniffing, she nodded.

"So you'll accept my gift?" Tucking his fingers beneath her chin, he lifted for a lingering glance into her eyes.

"Uh-huh."

They stood so close in ivy-laced shade it would take no effort to just lean in and kiss him. His warm breath, smelling of the chocolate chip cookies he'd downed with the kids for an after-story snack, caressed her lips.

It was a glorious summer day. Hot but bright and clear, filled with happy sounds of children laughing. Bees buzzing. Birds chirping. Sprinkler swishing.

Pulse pounding.

Whew. Removing her hands from Travis's remarkable chest, Kit shoved them into the hair at her temples. This wasn't happening. Mere weeks before her wedding, she wasn't devastatingly attracted to another man.

"We, uh…" She licked her aching lips. "We

should get back to work. Chrissy and Steph could probably use our help."

"It's recess. What's there to do but sit at the picnic table, soaking up sun?"

"You know kids," she said, already hustling away from him, out of the shady privacy they'd just shared. "Always up to something."

"What're you running from?" he asked loud enough for only her to hear.

"I'm not doing this," she said.

"What? Answering my simple question?"

Spinning around, tennis shoes crunching the driveway's gravel, she countered, "Simple, huh? Like that question you asked the night Levi almost walked in on us kissing?"

"You wanted to kiss me."

"Yes, but it was a mistake," she said. "One I'm horribly sorry about."

"But you just couldn't help yourself?"

"Hush," she said in the same curt tone she used on unruly children. "You're incorrigible. And the worst part is, you don't care. You're an unmanageable wild child only out for a good time. You couldn't care less who ends up getting hurt in the process."

"You're dead wrong." Grasping her upper arm, he said, "I care a helluva lot. Especially if you're this easily swayed by my supposed bad influence—it might be an indicator you're making a mistake."

"I can't hear you," she said, wrenching free, storming off with her hands over her ears.

"And so what if I am unmanageable? Seems to me that's part of my charm. The fact that you can't control me."

"La, la, la…" she sang, hands clamped tight but not nearly tight enough to drown the whole of his words. Yes, he was exciting. In her heart of hearts, he excited the hell out of her. When they'd been sixteen, his kisses made her want to break every rule she'd ever been given. Those kisses had left her fevered and achy and craving base things she shouldn't have even known about yet seriously explored. Things like getting her swollen breasts laved and suckled. And like guiding Travis's all-too-willing hands to that mysterious need between her legs. It was destroying her that after all the years between them, all the vows she'd made to never look at her best friend's brother in a romantic light again, he could do so little to bring their magic crashing back.

But like him, that magic was an illusion.

As soon as he got custody of Libby—which, in light of Beulah's stunt, he surely would—he'd be gone. Meanwhile, warm, safe and solid Levi would still be here, ready to unwittingly pick up the pieces of her broken heart. Which made her feel like the world's biggest witch. She didn't even deserve Levi's goodness. So what if he worked all the time? He was working for her. To save money for their future home and family. And for that, she owed him everything. Above all, her loyalty and promise to be faithful only unto him.

So with her hands still over her ears, she marched straight to the daycare's back door.

"And you call me a child?" Travis asked, following her inside when, unfortunately, the children and their two teachers were still outside. "Running off like that, right in the middle of a conversation."

"A conversation that we never should've had," she snapped. "I adore Levi. He's a caring, giving man. And no matter what you say, I am going to marry him in just three weeks' time."

"And you love him?"

"Of course," she said, notching her chin higher.

"That's all I wanted to know."

"Okay." Hands trembling from the depths of emotion coursing through her, she crossed her arms, willing herself to breathe. Everything would be all right. Yes, she'd been sorely tempted by Travis, but she hadn't followed through with her ridiculous feelings. Her vows to be true to Levi were intact.

Ha! her conscience taunted.

She might've been faithful in the physical sense. But in her heart? That was an entirely different matter.

Chapter Thirteen

"Nervous?"

Travis glanced up from the marble courthouse lobby bench to see Levi stroll his way. "A little," Travis said, straightening the knot on his tie. "If there's one thing I've learned in business, it's not to count chickens before they hatch. Especially with an adversary like Beulah."

"Kit told me about the woman's flyer." Chuckling, he made the universal sign for cuckoo alongside his head. "Seriously, though, I've known Beulah all my life, and she's actually a pretty good gal. Just takes a while to grow on you."

"Like a big, hairy mole," Travis said with a grunt.

Kit hustled in, smoothing her straight-lined black suit. Travis had never seen her dressed like this—like a woman from his world, if he even knew where that was anymore. She looked lovely but in a cool, almost cruel way. With her hair pulled severely back, she wasn't herself. His stomach tightened with wanting for the old Kit. The coltish teen who'd dazzled him wearing not much more than frayed jean shorts and ratty old T-shirts. The comely woman with fitted peasant-style tops and soft, flowing skirts she wore simply yet elegantly with sandals. Her long wavy hair swinging free for chubby infant fingers to explore.

Travis swallowed hard, wishing it weren't his own fingertips itching from the same need to know her top to bottom, inside and out.

"I'm so glad I'm not late," she said, slightly out of breath, her complexion healthy and glowing. "Steph has strep, so I had to find a last-minute replacement."

"She going to be okay?" Travis asked, having never had the misfortune of contracting the supposedly painful illness.

"Oh, sure. Once she's a few doses into her antibiotic, she'll be fine. Libby's good, too. She and Clara were having a raspberry war, apparently trying to judge who was loudest—our goddaughter's winning. So, see? It's you I'm worried about," she said, hand centered on his back in what he supposed was meant to have been a comforting gesture but in actuality made him acutely uncomfortable. "How're you holding up?"

He'd been better.

He didn't like being with Levi and Kit when they were together.

Seeing them as a couple reminded him how alone he was. Sure, he had Libby, but who else?

When he'd first come to IdaBelle Falls as a teen,

he recalled feeling as if he were part of a family. But this time around, in sparring with Beulah, he'd set himself apart as the outsider. The enemy. And if for some reason the judge ruled against him? Then what? What was he supposed to do with the rest of his life, knowing that while he'd had his sister, he'd wasted their brief time being sullen and hurt over her not having chosen his course? Who was to say which of them had been right?

Or whether there even was a right and a wrong or just different choices.

If only Marlene could hear him Upstairs, he'd want her to know how deeply sorry he was for not having been more supportive of whatever paths she'd chosen for her life.

"Travis?" Kit gave him a nudge. "Hello? Anyone home?"

"Sorry," he said with a start. "Just thinking."

"About how good it'll feel to get Libby back to Chicago?" Levi asked.

"Yeah…" Funny, that's what should've been on his mind. Purposely avoiding looking at Kit, Travis said, "It'll be good to be home."

Beulah and her entourage of blue-haired ladies wandered in, along with Gary's father, who walked over to shake his hand. "May the best *parent* win."

"Thank you," Travis said.

"For the record," the older man said with a glance over his shoulder toward his wife, "Beulah's tired. She loves Libby more than life itself, but she's not in the best of health and, off the record, I think it'd be in her best interest to start settling down."

Not sure what to say, Travis mumbled another thank you, then followed his attorney, who'd been talking on his cell, into the already crowded courtroom.

"What were you doing talking to him?" Travis overheard Beulah complain.

"Why are you going through with this?" Frank asked.

"Because it wasn't supposed to get this far."

"What's that mean?"

Teeth clenched, muscle popping in his jaw, Travis took a seat at his legal team's assigned table.

For a split second he shut his eyes, wondering to what extent his life was about to change. If Libby was his to take, he would go. If the judge ruled it in her best interest to stay? Travis would stay. And fight. Fight till he ran out of money and breath. For the one thing he'd learned during his time in this one horse town was that he very much wanted to be a father in every sense of the word.

"Hey," Kit said, bending over the oak rail separating the business end of the somber oak-paneled room from the gallery. She'd said the word in his ear, the warm, throaty vibration rocketing frissons of inappropriate awareness through him. "I forgot to wish you luck."

"Thanks," he said, wondering if just the smallest bit of her wanted him to lose, forcing him to stay. Or was that him doing the wondering? Was it him wanting to know if, in the event he did stay, things would change between them? Would she call off her wedding to Levi to pursue feelings he wasn't just imagining still simmered between them?

AFTER A TEDIOUS YET incredibly stressful morning of testimony from seemingly everyone with an opinion in the whole stinking town, the judge called a lunch recess, then lumbered from the courtroom.

Meanwhile, Travis wandered into the lobby to stretch his legs.

Time seemed frozen. With everyone else scurrying off to find a meal or run a quick errand, the space felt cavernous. Lonely. A part of him was relieved Kit had long since vanished. Another part felt as anxious as the dogs who got all riled up expecting the mailman, only to find out the noise they heard was just an ordinary passing car. Still, he couldn't stop glancing up each time someone new entered the lobby.

When finally Kit did appear, Travis found himself irrationally angry she'd been gone. "That was pretty intense," she said without her usual grin.

"You thought it wouldn't be?" Why was he upset with her? Maybe he resented her sitting in the gallery beside her fiancé rather than beside him. But then, to have sat next to him, Kit would have to have been his wife. That he could even think such a thing told him what this morning—the past few weeks—had done to his sanity!

"Sorry," he said, wanting to pull her into his arms, draw comfort from her strength, seeing how he felt as if the proceedings had drained any he might've had.

"Apology accepted." She cast him a smile akin to healing sun. "And it might interest you to know that, according to old Ben down at the hardware store, these are selling like hotcakes." Hand on her jacket's lapels, she flashed him, revealing a scandalously tight black T-shirt that read in bold white block letters: Team Uncle Travis.

"You've got to be kidding me," Travis said with a groan. "Levi's actually selling those?"

"Well…it's actually the IdaBelle Falls Pom Squad. They're trying to raise money for a trip to San Antonio. Jenny Calhoun's dad owns the Quick Copy, and often prints up T-shirts, too. Anyway, all profits go to a good cause. I hear the girls are awesome this year."

Shaking his head, Travis just headed back into the courtroom. What could he say? His normally staid, structured-to-the-minute life had been shot to hell, and there wasn't a damned thing anyone could do about it.

"Travis," Kit said, hot on his trail, "if the shirt bothers you, I can take it off. I just thought it might encourage you to know not everyone in this town sides with Beulah. In fact, your shirts are outselling hers two to one."

"Great."

How was he supposed to feel better seeing two of Beulah's blue-haired posse storm the courtroom aisle in hot pink Team Granny Beulah T-shirts.

"Travis?" Kit said, her voice soft and laced with concern.

"Yeah?"

Her big green eyes were wide. "It's just my opinion, but I think you'll make a great dad. I'm sure the judge will think so, too."

God help him, but Travis couldn't stop himself from pulling her into his arms. Her words meant the world. Having Kit think he was doing all right by Libby was the equivalent of earning the *Good Housekeeping* Seal of Approval.

"I love you," she said, palms pressed flat against his back. "Like the brother I never had."

"I love you, too," he said, pressing a chaste kiss into her hair. *But not anything like a sister.* "Thanks for being here."

"There's nowhere I'd rather be."

"All rise!" the bailiff shouted.

The shuffling of feet and the crying of a baby accompanied the judge's return to the room. After he glared in the general vicinity of the squalling child, the woman jiggling the blue-bootied noisemaker hopped up from her bench seat and hustled outside.

"Now, then," Judge Hobart Washington said, taking an eternity to get settled behind the bench, then shuffled a thick stack of papers. "Where were we?"

Where we are, Travis thought with a grimace, *is sitting here, heart racing, palms sweating, mouth dry.* Until this very moment Travis hadn't realized how dearly he wanted Libby to be permanently his. He wanted to take her sailing on glistening Lake Michigan on that boat he had yet to buy. He wanted her to grow up in the fairy-tale castle of his family home, only he wanted the place filled to the rafters with folks she loved. Trouble was, at the moment it was just the two of them. But he could change that. He wasn't sure how, but his whole life, once he'd set his mind to wanting something, be it an achievement or another tangible thing, he'd had it, won it, bought it.

Great plan, bud. Only problem is, Kit's not for sale. And she's the one you want to help fill your castle, right?

Wrong. Chicago was brimming with suitable candidates.

He glanced over his shoulder to find Kit gazing at him with such intensity he feared his heart might bust. It might not be manly, but it was true. He wanted out of this courtroom. He wanted Libby cradled in one arm, and the other slipped around Kit's waist. And he wanted his dogs. All three smelly, hairy, barking beasts. And—

"Ah, yes, Mrs. Redding," the judge boomed in a deep baritone that'd make the most hardened bank robber think twice about stealing another dime. Beulah, on the other hand, just straightened in her chair, not intimidated one iota by the black man's imposing size or commanding presence. "Is it true you distributed this flyer to each and every businessperson in and within a ten-mile radius of IdaBelle Falls?"

The hearing thus far had been casual in that neither

party had been put on the stand. But when Beulah's legal representative tried answering the question for her, the judge ordered the man to be quiet.

"I'm waiting," the judge again directed to Beulah. "Did you or did you not distribute the flyers?"

"Yes sir, I did."

The judge wrote and wrote, then said to Travis and Beulah, "I must say, I've already formed an opinion on this matter based upon the increasingly flimsy basis of your contesting of your son's will. However, in the interest of the infant at the heart of this hearing, I would like to hear from each of you why, in your most earnest, heartfelt words, you feel it would benefit Libby Callahan-Redding to reside within your respective homes. Mrs. Redding, ladies first."

"Thank you, Your Honor." Rising, Beulah cleared her throat, used a tissue to dab the corners of her heavily made-up eyes. "I suppose what I have to offer my granddaughter might not be all that special to someone like Travis Callahan, but to my son and to Mr. Callahan's own sister, this *something* obviously meant a great deal." She took a deep shuddering breath. "That something is the small-town way of life. The notion that no one in IdaBelle Falls is ever alone. That we're all God's children and here to help one another in every—"

"That why you told everyone in town to refuse my business, Beulah? That why—"

"Mr. Callahan," the judge called out, "kindly wait your turn."

It might not have been his turn, but Travis wasn't about to take Beulah's sticky-sweet pack of lies sitting down. How could she have already forgotten the flyer the judge had just referenced? Bolting from his chair, Travis slapped his palms on the table. "Tell me, Beulah, were those flyers supposed o help instill welcoming and warm fuzzies for me throughout this supposedly fine, upstanding community?"

"Mr. Callahan!" the judge bellowed.

"I only asked them to make things hard enough for you that not only would you *have* to stay in town but maybe you'd turn to a special someone for support. And then, if I was lucky, you and Kit might—"

A collective gasp came from the gallery.

"Order!" The judge slammed his gavel on the bench. Travis sat.

"Thank you, Mr. Callahan. Now, Mrs. Redding, assuming I didn't just hear you essentially confess this hearing has been nothing more than a game. Begin again. This time from the heart."

Beulah sniffled, started dabbing her eyes again.

"Anytime," the judge urged. "This court has a very full docket."

"My deep-down reasons for wanting to keep Libby are intensely personal, Your Honor. I loved my only son. Dearly. Burying him was harder than anything I could possibly imagine—other than the idea of his precious, beloved baby girl moving away from me, never to be seen again. And that's it. The whole enchilada.

"I know full well that in the event of tragedy my son and his wife wanted Travis to raise their baby girl. I'm too old to tackle Libby's daily care. Knowing that, I did the second best thing by trying to make Travis see what a wonderful place IdaBelle Falls is to raise a family, although I realize my methods were questionable. I know I can't make him fall for Kit Wells, the infant's godmother, any more than I can make him care for our sweet town. But don't you think I at least owed it to myself—and my granddaughter—to try?"

Travis glanced over his shoulder to see Levi clenching his jaw.

"Simply stated," Beulah continued, "I don't think I could survive losing my son, then losing my granddaughter, as well.

"Honestly...since I am under oath," she said, glancing Travis's way, "each time I've paid him and Libby a visit, he's been doing a fine job. He's in no way the misfit I'd anticipated him to be. But just because I don't find him objectionable to be around doesn't mean I think he should run off to Chicago.

"A-and that's all. I'm sorry, Travis. I thought I had everything all worked out to benefit everyone, but..." Snatching a fresh tissue from her husband's outstretched hand, Beulah noisily blew her nose before retaking her seat.

"Thank you, Mrs. Redding. I'm sorry if that was painful, but both I and this court appreciate your candor." Turning to Travis, Judge Washington said, "Mr. Callahan, on behalf of Barker County and

IdaBelle Falls, I apologize for having wasted your valuable time." To Beulah he said, "Mrs. Redding, I assume you've kept a record of payments you've made to various businesses around town. I would like each of those payments returned and a formal apology written to Mr. Callahan by each of the proprietors giving our fair city a bad name by having taken such bribes. Furthermore, should you ever so much as think about taking legal matters into your own hands again, Mrs. Redding, rest assured I will personally see to it you're punished to the full extent of the law."

"Travis Callahan," the judge decreed, "I hereby grant you sole custody of your niece as stated in the terms of her parents' last will and testament."

Travis's heart stopped.

Beulah choked back a sob.

The gallery erupted.

Only then did Travis dare breathe. He'd won. Libby had won. But gazing at the infant's distraught grandmother—the woman who clearly adored the baby girl and vice versa—Travis realized the only thing gained by keeping Beulah out of Libby's life was a tactical victory.

Doing what he hoped his sister and brother-in-law would've wanted him to do, he forgave the woman for ever having toyed with him, then he marched into the heart of enemy territory, olive branch in hand, making it clear she and Frank would always be a welcome addition to Libby's life.

THAT AFTERNOON, THOUGH Kit's hands were busy assembling roast-beef-and-Swiss sandwiches in Travis's modern kitchen, her mind and heart were still reeling. She'd tried talking with Levi about what happened in court, but he'd had to work. Kit had expected him to be shocked by Beulah's words, but he'd just shrugged, claiming things had obviously turned out the way they were supposed to. But had they really?

Travis was leaving, taking the child she'd grown to love with him.

What about the man? Do you love him, too?

Worrying her lower lip, she decided that the jury was still out on that subject.

Setting Travis's plate on the table in front of him and a few slices of chopped beef and cheese on gurgling Libby's high-chair tray, Kit said, "I'm glad it came out that Beulah was bribing all those folks to deny you service. This really is a great town."

"Not like Chicago." His pushed back his chair on his way to the fridge, where he pulled out a near-empty jar of Beulah's prizewinning bread-and-butter pickles. "Can you even imagine how many cultural opportunities Libby might've missed?"

"Yeah, well…" Kit tried coming up with a comparable retort but was flat out. Honestly what *did* IdaBelle Falls offer that Chicago couldn't? What had Marlene found so darn fascinating about this town? True, it was safe. And a certain comfort came from knowing most everyone you ran across. But, fundamentally, was it the place that made somewhere a home or was it the people with whom you shared it? Funny how when she'd thought there was even the smallest hope of Travis staying, the small town had been her whole world, but now that it was clear he was leaving, IdaBelle Falls felt suffocating. "I am happy for you," she somehow managed. "I know you're eager to get back to your office."

Taking a bite of the pickle-laden sandwich, he nodded.

"What are you going to do about Libby? You know, as far as daycare?"

"Actually," he said after swallowing his latest bite, "I've given it a lot of thought and I want to cut way back on my workload to spend as much time as possible with her."

Pleasantly surprised, Kit raised her eyebrows.

"No need to look shocked. In a roundabout way, Beulah did me a favor in forcing me to stay. If I hadn't, I probably would've gone on believing Rose Industries wouldn't last a day without me. But I've got good people onboard. The company's in capable hands. It's a huge relief knowing those hands don't always have to be mine. Meaning—" he interlocked his fingers with hers "—I'll be back for plenty of visits. Now that I've given this place at least a partial face-lift, it's started feeling more like home. Although, there's still a lot I'd like to do."

Reeling from the news Travis wouldn't be completely, cleanly out of her life, Kit said the first thing that popped into her mind that didn't involve her overloaded feelings.

"Can I make a suggestion?"

"Shoot."

"How about remodeling the shed into an office, then turning the front parlor back into the grand space your sister always meant it to be?"

He laughed.

"I'm serious. Think about it. Libby's not going to be a baby forever. How do you think she'll feel bringing friends home to that?" She gestured toward the general vicinity of the ugly high-tech space.

"Why do you even care?" he asked. "Libby and I will only be here part-time. And it's not like you're stuck living here."

But I'd like to be.

Ugh. Kit put her hands over her face.

What was wrong with her? She wasn't a melodramatic teen anymore, tossed into a fit of despair over Travis's leaving. So why did she have a massive knot in her throat?

"No, I'm not living here," she said, "but it's the principle of the thing. Libby shouldn't grow up in an office. This should be her home."

"And, again, for the brief time she's here, I hope she'll consider it a home. But seeing how she now has many homes, I fail to see what you're so upset about. Didn't you get the memo? We won."

"I know. Excuse me but, about the house, I'm trying to be helpful. In case you've forgotten, a lot was at stake for me today, too. I love Libby as if she were my own. And if you want to know the truth, I secretly wanted her—and you—to stay. So there, I said it. And I feel horrible about it. But there it is, out on the table. If you never want to speak to me again, I—"

"Why didn't you want me to leave?" he quietly asked. "Was it just because you'd miss seeing Libby every day? Or something more?"

She bowed her head, wishing he lacked the unsettling ability to see right through her. Or did he? If he really did know what resided in the innermost depths of her heart, he wouldn't have even needed to ask the question.

Lord help her, but she loved him.

But how could she love him and marry Levi? She loved him, too. Only, more and more, she feared her love for him wasn't an apples-to-apples comparison. More like apples to pineapples. But then, hadn't she long ago determined Travis was intrinsically bad for her? They hadn't worked out as teens. Who was to say they'd work out now? Maybe it wasn't him she loved at all, but Marlene and Libby and anything she felt for Travis was just illusion, tough to see through her still-strong grief.

What she'd shared with Travis had been amazing but fleeting. The way things had ended between them had hurt to the point that she was now terrified of going through the same thing all over again—only this time she'd lose Libby, too, if Travis were to decide marriage wasn't for him, not that he'd even broached the subject.

Sure, he'd asked her that one time to break up with Levi, but he'd never said why. Did he want to date her? Marry her? Merely sleep with her? How could she be sure he'd even been serious? If he had been, she couldn't emotionally put herself out there that way, which was why she had to squash her attraction to Travis like a bug. Nothing good could come from a relationship forged on a foundation of fear. Yes, he'd changed, improved, apologized, but none of that mattered. The only thing she could do was listen to the warning bells telling her to keep a safe distance.

"Kit? I asked a fairly straightforward question. You ever planning to answer?"

"No," she said, hating the gossamer weakness of her voice. "I'm not going to answer because there's no mystery to my statement. Obviously I have strong feelings for both you and Libby. For her I feel love. For you, deep friendship. Which is why I hope you'll at least not take off right away but stay through to the wedding."

Chapter Fourteen

"For what it's worth," Beulah said in Travis's sun-flooded kitchen the Sunday afternoon after the hearing, "I'm sorry. For everything. Most especially for your sister's passing. She was a good girl. A great mother." She stood at the white marble counter wiping the sprinkling of flour still left from a batch of oatmeal cookies she'd made earlier.

Libby in his arms, Travis wasn't sure what to think of her statement. He wanted to believe she truly was sorry, but on the flip side, had he been in her position, wouldn't he have gone to any measure to keep what he felt was rightfully his? "If I haven't before mentioned it," he said, "I'm sorry about your son. I hardly knew him, but he seemed like a good guy. He was always kind to Marlene. She adored him."

"Gary *was* a good son. He loved Marlene and Libby very much. In fact, the few times I've seen you and Kit together, you two reminded me of your sister and my son. Which is why I thought it only logical you end up together. Well, that and I knew you used to be sweet on each other when you were younger. You like her, don't you?"

"Sure I like her," he said with a laugh. "Everyone *likes* Kit. Kids, dogs—" me "—everyone."

"Son, do you honestly think for one second you're pullin' the wool over my eyes?"

"In what regard?" he asked, getting the bow he'd been trying to tie on Libby's bib wound into a doozy of a knot.

She snorted. "You keep deluding yourself right up to the wedding day, you're going to lose her."

"Who said I wanted her? I mean, beyond as a friend."

She popped the top on a jar of baby peaches. "Not that I'm one to put my nose in other folks' business, but mark my words, if you don't tell the girl how you feel, you'll regret it for the rest of your life."

"Beulah, I might not have told her in so many words how I feel, but I did flat-out tell her she should call off this engagement before she winds up making a lifelong mistake."

"What'd she say?"

"Called me an ass."

Shaking her head, the older woman clicked her tongue. "Sure sign a woman's in love—only she doesn't know it. More logical—doesn't care to admit it."

"No way. I've given her plenty of opportunity to come clean with me about her true feelings."

"When you say *opportunities,* did you hem and haw or did you come right out and confess how much you care for her, *then* ask her if she feels the same?"

Travis scratched his head.

"Son, that's what I thought. You might've thought you told her, but you didn't really. I'm telling you now, if you're to have a flying frog's chance at regaining the girl's affection, you're going to have to tell her the truth in no uncertain terms."

"What if she just ends up calling me names again?"

"Well, at least you'll have the satisfaction of knowing you tried."

"FABULOUS!" WORLD-RENOWNED photographer Betty Anne Worshire shouted over a pulsing Aerosmith CD. "Work it, Miss Kitty!"

"I'm trying," Kit shouted right back. "But don't you think this pose is a little…much?" On this sunny mid-August afternoon, blue sky dazzling, the purported genius had Kit—decked out in full bridal regalia—perched on what would in photos appear to be a simple wooden swing hanging alongside thundering IdaBelle Falls. Trouble was, it wasn't a swing she was on but a crane suspended twenty feet in the air!

Granted, Betty Anne knew her business. But what didn't she get about Kit being a small-town girl who was marrying a small-town guy in what was supposed to have been a simple small-town wedding with equally simple photos?

"There's no such thing as *too much,* dahling! Now work it! Work it! Give me raw sex appeal! Bridal lust!"

Kit tried her best, but seeing how Levi was away at a wrench-and-socket convention, it'd been a few days since she'd even had a kiss, let alone felt anything closely resembling lust.

Then she spotted Travis, dressed more casually than she'd ever seen him in khaki cargo shorts and a navy Rose Industries T-shirt. He hadn't shaved, his dark hair was a mess and dark sunglasses covered his eyes. Leaning against an oak, arms crossed, muscular biceps bulging, she'd also never seen him look more handsome. Not exactly at ease but at least looking as if he belonged in her world. Which was good, considering he'd promised to stay a short while longer.

The thought made her sad yet happy.

The night after the hearing, she and Levi had relaxed at her place and watched a movie. It had been exactly what she needed. It had reminded her that while her fiancé might not be adept at scintillating conversation, he was great at holding and soothing her without having to tell her with words that everything would be okay.

Yes, Travis was handsome and witty, but based on their history, he wasn't marriage material. Just the stuff of dreams that would slowly, bit by bit, fade away.

In the meantime, she thought, giving Travis one last lingering glance, she'd enjoy him as a friend, knowing that with Levi beside her, she'd have the strength when the time came to say a final goodbye—if not physically for the last time, at least in her heart where it most mattered.

"Perfect!" Betty Anne called out. "Yes! Loving that wistful longing for your man!"

WHILE HIS GOOD FRIEND Betty Anne and her crew set up for the next shot, Travis wandered toward the bride where she'd temporarily parked on the edge of a tall black director's chair. "You looked gorgeous up there on that swing."

"Thanks," she said, gazing to her lap, where she held her hands close, fidgeting with pearls on her skirt.

"What were you thinking during that last shot?"

"What do you mean?" she asked, gazing up but not really meeting his eyes.

"The question was straightforward enough. Were you remembering a great date with Levi? Some buck-wild hot night?"

"Travis," she said, laughing. "What am I going to do with you?"

"I'm pretty sure at this point," he said with a grin, "I'm too old to teach any new tricks."

"Incorrigible. That's what you are."

He captured her delicate hand against his chest, hoping she couldn't feel his erratic pulse. While his growing feelings for Kit hadn't changed, witnessing her happy glow as she anticipated her big day convinced him to ignore Beulah's advice to tell Kit how much she meant to him. How much she'd always meant. He didn't want to think he'd fallen for the unattainable. Didn't want to believe. But being up close and personal to Kit like this was never easy. If they were solely friends, shouldn't horsing around and joking be all in a day's fun? Why did everything she said have a bittersweet tone? And why, when he saw her in the dress she'd wear to marry another man, did he keep fighting crazy, childish urges to douse her in grape Kool-Aid or red and orange finger paint, and ruin the pricey garment? "When you're done," he asked, hating himself, "you wanna hang out?"

"Sure, but don't you have to get Libby from Beulah's?"

"Not till eight. Besides, we've got something to celebrate." He held her hand, then settled his palm against it, easing his fingers between hers, loving the feel and fit.

"Oh, yeah?" she said with an easy grin. "What's that?"

"Before picking you up, I was doing the books this morning and the Sycmore daycare is now running at capacity. Won't be too long before profits start creeping higher."

"That's great," she said. "Promise you're not kidding?"

"Have you ever known me to kid about money?" He winked.

She tossed her arms around him in a happy hug. "This is fantastic. You're a miracle worker. Why didn't Marlene bring you onboard years ago?"

I think we both know the answer to that.

Because once, on a rare visit to Chicago, while foraging for CD player batteries in Travis's dresser, Marlene had come across a picture of sixteen-year-old Kit. She'd asked him about it and he'd blown it off. Even though neither had ever mentioned it again, he'd gotten the feeling she'd intuitively sensed the photo meant more to him than just a casual memento. Never having been the sentimental type, he didn't keep ticket stubs from special dates or wedding invitations. He sure didn't keep snapshots lying around or tucked into the edges of dresser mirrors.

Marlene had then volunteered the fact that, all these years later, Kit was still ticked at him for breaking off their relationship without being man enough to say a word. He'd pointed out that he hadn't been a man but a stupid kid. Marlene said it didn't matter. He'd been a coward—and still was when it came to dealing with women. What she'd forgotten was that he'd been hurt, too. Finding out Natalie had been cheating on him had been no picnic. It was one more reason he was loathe to follow Beulah's advice. He may not think Levi was right for Kit, but he didn't want to be the guy who stole her from Levi, either. Now, if she came to him voluntarily, that would be a whole other story.

Marlene had confessed that, once, after a few too many piña coladas, she'd told Kit about the photo and how she suspected her brother had pined for her a good long while.

"A couple years ago," he said, still holding tight to her hand, "Marlene called me a coward when it came to women. You think that's true?"

"What brought that on?" she asked.

"Just answer the question. And please be honest."

"What does it matter what I think?"

"Then it's true?"

"Only you can answer that. What's your heart telling you?"

"My heart?" He laughed. "I wasn't aware it had a voice."

She rolled her eyes.

"No, seriously, Kit, watching you up there on that swing, all decked out in your pretty dress, got me to thinking. Am I ever going to find my own bride? A best friend for me and a mom for Libby?"

"Th-that depends," she said, lightly stroking his palm with her thumb. "Do you want to find such a woman? If so, I can get you a list of at least ten who'd love to date you."

"You could?" Did she have to volunteer her help so fast? What did it mean that she was so eager to have him off the open market?

"Gosh, yes. Just say the word and it's done."

"Think you could get me a date for the wedding?"

"I—I suppose so."

"Cool." *Because there's no way in hell I can watch you walk down that aisle on my own.*

"Miss Kitty?" Betty Anne called. "Ready for your next shot?"

"COME ON, GUYS," KIT SAID Friday night, holding up her latest risqué bridal shower gift—a red teddy trimmed in black feathers. "Don't you think we could use at least one toaster?"

Chrissy and Steph laughed, as did the other co-workers and friends from the now-thriving daycares. The one *friend* she missed sharing in her fun was Travis. Probably just as well in light of her unreadable feelings where he was concerned. Was he just a friend? Or more? One thing was for certain—due to her pending nuptials, she'd never grant herself permission to delve deeper.

"You'll be so hot in that number," Steph shouted, "Levi could fry an egg on your flat stomach!"

That earned still more roars.

After opening package after package of lace-and-feather get-ups, along with a few gag gifts like edible panties, Kit was exhausted—in a good way!

Long after the X-rated cake had been eaten and the last of the paper cups and plates and napkins and streamers thrown away, Kit found herself alone with Chrissy. While it felt comfortable working in tandem with the younger woman, their relationship was a long way from being the near-lifelong friendship she'd shared with Marlene. Still, Chrissy had been there for her a lot lately, helping with the flowers and even trekking to Little Rock with her to select the perfect dress.

"Nice party," Chrissy said.

"I thought so, but judging by this pile of adult paraphernalia, I'm thinking our friends are in serious need of male companionship."

Chuckling and fingering a white feather boa, Chrissy said, "No kidding. Marlene was always saying the same thing. She'd have liked this tonight," she added. "I miss her a lot."

The two shared a hug, then finished the cleanup job. Chrissy said her goodbyes, leaving Kit alone with far too many thoughts about the future and past.

Josh Groban softly playing on the stereo, she approached the mantel, tracing Levi's outline in their smiling engagement photo that'd been taken three years earlier.

Three long years.

Thirteen years since her summer with Travis. Ancient history. The closer the wedding came, the more determined she was to focus on her groom.

Levi was a wonderful, warm, funny, sweet man she'd be lucky to spend the rest of her life with. He loved her and they shared the same values and goals.

Travis was unobtainable. In her life for but a moment, seldom to be seen or heard from again.

The doorbell pealed, causing her to jump.

Levi?

Hoping so, she ran to the door, only to find Travis and Libby, both sporting grins.

"Surprise," he said, tickling Libby under her arm so she'd hold out a beautifully wrapped pink foil box. Only, his plan backfired when, instead of offering the gift, the darling baby gummed it. "So much for that," he said, landing an indulgent kiss to the cooing infant's head.

"She looks darling," Kit said, stepping aside for them both to come in. He'd dressed her in a pink taffeta dress and matching hair bow, pink patent-leather shoes and tights. "Someone's been shopping."

"Guilty," he said, closing the door on the night's muggy heat. "What can I say, I'm a sucker for a pretty girl needing new party duds. Speaking of which, how'd it go?"

"My shower?" On her way to the sofa she spun to face him, only that wasn't such a bright idea, seeing how that gave her a perfect view of his rock-hard abs and chest, covered in a starched cobalt button-down that smelled crisp and clean and made his eyes all the more intense. And those wide, wide shoulders. And— she looked up to his dear face. To lips she wanted to kiss so bad the wanting alone was tantamount to being unfaithful to her betrothed. Guilt slammed hard and fast, and she hastily took Libby from him, then backed away, perching on the sofa's far end. "It was a lot of fun but not entirely suitable for a girl of Libby's tender age."

"Hearing some of Chrissy and Steph's preplanning for the affair, I figured as much." He landed on the sofa's opposite end. "Well? I'm sure you're tired, so go ahead. Open your gift."

Gingerly taking it from Libby, she said, "You've already given us too much."

"Yeah, but the photographs are for you and Levi both. Tonight was called a *bridal* shower, remember?

You had to have a gift all for you. Besides, this is from Libby. Go ahead," he said with a heartbreakingly handsome smile. "Open it."

"Travis…"

"That's my name," he softly said, again breaching her safety perimeter. "Quit wearing it out."

"But…"

She opened the box, and nestled sweet as you please on white satin was a pair of pearl-and-diamond earrings that literally took her breath away.

"A-are they real?" she asked after her initial gasp.

"You think I'd give you fakes?"

"I—I'm not sure what to think. Only that they're amazing. And too much. Way, way too much. Levi wouldn't understand."

"Sure he would, seeing how I asked his permission."

"When?"

"This afternoon."

"Oh."

Travis set the box on the counter behind her and withdrawing one earring, then the other, raised them to her ears, where he put them in. His knuckles brushing the sensitive skin of her neck, she had to remind her heart to beat. What gave her the right to marry one man while wanting, with every fiber of her being, just one simple kiss from another?

Heartache, that's what.

Travis had burned her. Bad. Folks say first love isn't real. It doesn't matter. Doesn't count. But their first loves hadn't been the great Travis Callahan. They hadn't known what it was like being held captive in his spell. Yes, he was back. And for a while anyway, he was staying. But that still didn't make him any more real. That didn't make him the kind of stable family man she'd searched her whole life to find.

"They look good on you," he said, stepping back as if to admire the view. "Only, you should wear your hair up, piled high and loose and wild. That way Levi could have fun taking it down."

"Levi?" She licked her lips, willing her heart back into action.

"Who else?" He grinned.

She died, hugging Libby close, her broken dreams of what might've been with Travis, closer.

A WEEK LATER, WHILE LIBBY was home snoozing with a teenage sitter, Travis was stuck at Kit and Levi's rehearsal dinner, deciding whether to nurse his broken heart with liquor or cheesecake when Levi wandered up, a buffalo wing to his lips.

"Can't tell you how much it's meant to me, man, having you cover for Kit at the daycare while she's put all this together."

"My pleasure," Travis said, following her in his peripheral vision as she hammed it up on the dance floor of Lovett's Steak and Shrimp House with Steph and Chrissy. Lord, she looked beautiful swaying to Prince's "Purple Rain" in a pale peach sundress that made the most of her tan. She'd worn her hair up and loose, allowing plenty of sexy tendrils to escape. The diamonds and pearls he'd given her shone in the dim light.

"Well, anyway," Levi said, "just couldn't let the night go by without telling you how much your friendship and more than generous gifts have meant—to us both."

Not sure what to say, considering the treachery lurking in his heart, Travis smiled and nodded while Levi went off in search of more wings.

"You never told her, did you?" Beulah asked.

Travis sighed. Liquor was definitely the way to go. "What's a guy have to do to find peace around here?"

"Not possible," she said. "Now, the way I see it, you have two options. Keep this matter to yourself. Pine your life away alone and depressed. Or tell her how you feel."

"Thus ensuring Levi spends the rest of his life alone and depressed?" Travis signaled to the waiter to bring him a fresh scotch and water.

"Elaborating on option two," she said, steamrolling his objections in her usual brazen manner, "tell her you love her. Tell her you'll die without her."

"But I won't."

"Men," she said with a huff, storming off to her blue-haired crew.

While most rehearsal dinners were for only the wedding party and close family, Levi being Levi had invited pretty damn near the entire town. The meal had been an all-you-can-eat buffet. The drinks, free-flowing. All of which should've equaled a good time. So why did Travis feel like hammered dog doo?

Betty Anne sauntered up, camera covering half her face.

The flash blinded him.

"Great candid," she said. "Did you try the mushroom caps? Divine." She flashed him again, then was off ambushing some other unsuspecting victim.

A slow, sad country song Travis didn't recognize filled the air with a poignancy he didn't want or need. His situation wasn't helped when the source of his troubles drifted his way, holding out her arms.

"How 'bout putting down that drink," she said, her words slightly slurred as if she'd had maybe one too many. "You haven't danced with me all night."

"Everyone else has," he said. The last thing on earth he wanted to do was take her into his arms in this very public place.

"But you're the one who matters," she said. "It's my night's goal to prove you're not all that hot."

"Really?" he said with a whistle. "Pretty lofty ambition."

"Tell me about it." She puffed a fallen lock of hair out from in front of her right eye. "I thought I'd gotten you completely out of my system years ago. But then you came back. Shot my resolve all to hell."

"Sorry," he said, scarcely believing his ears.

"I used to love you, you know. Everyone said it wasn't possible, but I knew."

"You didn't love me," he said. "You loved Levi. He's always been the guy for you."

"Nope." With her fingers she fished a cherry from her empty drink.

"Let me take that," he said, wrenching her now-empty green-apple martini glass from her hand. Thankfully no one else seemed interested in their scene. As much as Travis had prayed for exactly this admission from Kit, this wasn't the way he'd wanted it. In a drunken confession the night before her wedding. And just a few moments earlier she'd been hugging Levi. Her blathering was nothing more than just that—clearing the garbage from her past to make way for her bright future.

"Yep," she said. "I knew I loved you and then I was going to track you down and make you—" She got a horrible look on her face, then ran for the balcony door.

Chapter Fifteen

"I—I think I drank too much," Kit sputtered after what she hoped was the last of her dry heaves. She stood at the rail of the restaurant's deck that hung out over the Beaver River. Thank god she hadn't lost it right in the middle of the party. But then, wait—in her drunken rambling, she vaguely remembered spewing something far worse than what felt like her ten-odd drinks!

"You think?" Travis asked, handing her a cool cloth for her mouth, which she then put on her throbbing forehead.

"I don't recall asking your opinion." What was wrong with her? Why couldn't she have kept her big mouth shut?

"All I did was agree with you."

"Yeah, well—don't." Maybe he hadn't been paying attention. Or even better, maybe he hadn't even heard her; the music had been awfully loud.

"Want me to tell Levi you're ready to go?"

She shook her head. "I don't want him to see me like this."

"By this time tomorrow you'll be married to the guy. Don't you think over the next fifty, sixty years he'll see you throw up?"

"Is there a reason you're out here? Other than to harass me?"

"Nope," he said with a mocking whistled tune, feigning boredom. "That's pretty much my sole reason for being."

"Have I told you lately what a jerk you are?"

"Not in the last hour or so."

"Well, you—" Her stomach fisted, sending her back over the rail.

"Relax," Travis said, rubbing her back, easing warmth and reassurance through her aching nerve-shattered limbs. "That's it… Breathe deeply."

"I'm afraid," she said, leaning back against him.

"Of what? Being sick during the ceremony?"

She shook her head against the solid strength of his chest.

"Then what?"

That I'm making a huge mistake.

I'm marrying the wrong man.

Which was why she'd drunk nearly a pitcher of green-apple martinis! But hadn't she already been through this? Hadn't she long since determined Travis wasn't the settle-down, marrying type?

"Kit?" He stopped kneading her shoulders to gently turn her to face him. "What's on your mind?"

"Nothing," she said, head bowed. "It's stupid."

"If something's bothering you to this degree, obviously it's not stupid."

She nibbled her lower lip.

"Come on, lay it on me. Wedding jitters?"

She nodded.

"You've done a great job with the planning. No woman will ever have as beautiful a ceremony and reception as you."

"I know."

"And Levi's a great guy. The best. Plus, in marrying him, you've got a live-in plumber, lawn guy, HVAC guy and auto mechanic."

"He's not that good with cars."

"Okay, but he does all the rest, right?"

She nodded against Travis's chest, drinking in his warm strength, never wanting to let him go. Which only made her feel all the worse.

"Besides which, the guy clearly adores you." With his free arm he gestured inside to where the groom was singing karaoke with Chrissy, Steph and Beulah.

"You really think so?"

"I *know* so," he said, drawing her into his arms, kissing the top of her head and slow dancing to the crickets and the stars.

AFTER CHECKING ON LIBBY, standing under the shower till the water ran cold, drinking a Coke, then a beer, then another Coke and trying to sleep and failing, Travis now sat on the front porch. Under the same sky he'd shared with Kit just a couple hours earlier. Only now, it seemed different. More vast.

Telling Kit how much Levi loved her had cost Travis ten years of his life.

Up to that moment, he hadn't been sure if he'd take Beulah's advice in telling Kit his true feelings for her or not. Then he'd seen the look in Kit's eyes when she'd whispered Levi's name. She did love him. Travis knew if he truly loved her, he'd step out of the way and let the wedding go off the way it should. By her own admission, Travis had already hurt Kit bad. Why put her through that again when she would inevitably discover he wasn't built for long-lasting relationships and, since becoming CEO, had always put business before pleasure.

On the other hand, he'd changed. Look how great he was getting along with Libby. And lately, to his surprise, the last thing on his mind was work.

Cocoa wandered up, nuzzling her head under his palm.

And the dogs. He didn't even like dogs, yet look how they wanted to be with him.

Cocoa whined.

Travis hefted her up onto the swing beside him. The two other dogs were already there.

He couldn't tell Kit he loved her on the eve of her wedding. How many chances had he already had with her? Five? Ten? A couple dozen? And all those times he'd backed down. Why? Because deep in his heart he knew he was no good for her.

He didn't know the first thing about sustaining a relationship. Sure, he was a fantastic starter, but Kit deserved the total deluxe good-guy package. Although his grandparents had married young and stayed together till their deaths less than a year apart, they'd never been overly demonstrative as a couple. In fact, they'd often done their own thing, meeting up for occasional private diners. His parents' relationship had been a joke. Considering how much they fought, how they'd managed to stay married always had been a mystery to him.

With that history, what kind of future did he have? He'd be great with Libby because she was a kid. He remembered enough of his own childhood to bring her up the way he wished he'd been raised.

But marriage? Best he leave that to the experts— namely the couple getting hitched in the morning.

Which was why he booted the dogs off the swing, then corralled the whole lot of them into the house and turned off the lights and locked the door.

He had a big day tomorrow.

Starting with somehow reassembling the pieces of his shredded heart.

"YOU'RE BEAUTIFUL," KIT'S mother said. She and Kit's father had missed the rehearsal dinner due to their RV having a flat in Topeka. But they were here now, for which Kit was most grateful.

She needed an army of strength today. The day that was supposed to be the happiest of her life.

But all she seemed capable of thinking of was the fairy tale. The dreams she'd had as a little girl of strolling down the aisle toward a man who didn't so much make her feel comfortable and secure as *alive*. Tingly with excitement and anticipation for whatever surprises the future may hold.

Then she'd met Travis and, in her silly teen fantasies, thought for that brief shining time he'd been the one. How could she have been so wrong about him when to this day every bone in her body told her she was right? He was *the* one. Only, he wasn't, seeing how in under an hour she'd be strolling down the aisle toward Levi, who admittedly was a good friend, but was he the happily ever after?

Swallowing back tears, she reminded herself of her second failed attempt with Brad at finding that elusive dream.

When would she once and for all learn dreams were just for the third of her life she spent sleeping. Reality was what she needed to focus on. Creating a safe, secure haven in which to live the rest of her life. Working, raising children, keeping a peaceful, loving home. Those were her priorities now and always had been.

"It's been so long since Daddy and I have been in town," her mother said, fussing with Kit's veil, "I feel totally out of the loop."

"What do you want to know?" Kit volunteered, happy for the chance to get her mind on anything other than what might've been with Travis.

"For starters, where did you-all decide to go for your honeymoon?"

"Hot Springs," Kit said.

Her mother wrinkled her nose. "Don't get me wrong, it's a lovely town, but I thought you'd always wanted an exotic island getaway. Hawaii or some lush Caribbean resort?"

"I know," Kit said, gazing wistfully at her reflection in the church's antique cheval mirror that'd seen literally hundreds of brides before her and would, God willing, see hundreds after her, as well. How many had been jubilant? How many, like her, felt a strange unease? As if they were resigned to marry rather than elated by the prospect?

"So what happened?" Her mother cupped her hand to Kit's forearm. The small show of affection only made Kit's steely determination to choke back tears all the harder.

"Levi couldn't take the time away from the store." Forcing a breath and a bright smile, she added, "He promised we'd take a nice long trip somewhere fabulous soon."

"Oh, well..."

That pretty much summed up Kit's thoughts on the matter.

Funny how all along, she'd assumed Travis was a business warrior, when he'd virtually abandoned his Chicago operations to take over here, where he was needed. Would Levi have done the same? Put family ahead of business? Or would the store always come first for him, family second?

"LOOKS LIKE I GOT MY money's worth," Travis mumbled, parking the new black SUV he'd bought when the daycare van's engine bit the big one toward the back of the stone chapel's dirt lot. The place was idyllic. Straight out of an ivy-encrusted fairy tale. Heavy festoons of white orchids and lilies and roses and ferns and more ivy lined the stone railings and arched double doors.

He could've gotten a date for the ordeal, but why? He'd only be making the day harder on himself by having to entertain someone when all he wanted to do was go home and hide.

Libby cooed and gurgled in her safety seat while Travis unlatched her harness, then fluffed her pink ruffled skirt and refastened her pink Velcro bow, which had fallen onto her car seat tray.

"Glad one of us is happy about being here," he said, patting his chest pocket to find his final gift to Kit still there.

Libby held securely in the crook of his right arm, Travis closed up the SUV and began the long march to the chapel, cringing each time he had to return a smile and wave. Never had he wished more to be back in Chicago, where the sheer numbers of people ensured anonymity.

"Fine day for a wedding, isn't it?" Bruce Calhoun of Quick Copy said, gesturing for Travis to lead up the stairs. Beneath his suit coat he wore a T-shirt reading Married People Have More Fun!

"Sure is," Travis somehow said, doubting the shirt's

sentiment. "The bride and groom couldn't have paid for better weather." The sky was clear and vivid blue. The temperature, after nighttime storms, fresh and cool.

Steeling his shoulders, clutching Libby tight, Travis mounted the steps. He wanted this wedding to take place. Above all, even more than he wanted Kit for himself, he wanted her to be happy. And if she were with him, he knew she could never be. He would one day return to Chicago. Then what? How many times had she, by her own admission, said she could never live in a big city? How many times had she said she'd feel lost?

Yes, but if I were there to hold your hand, then—

"I take it you still haven't told her?" Beulah swished up behind him in a perfumed cloud of yellow satin and lace, taking Libby from him. "I never took you for a big ole fraidy cat, Travis Callahan."

Ignoring her, enormously grateful she'd taken Libby, leaving him only himself to care for on this most crappy of days, Travis entered the chapel, sickened by the overwhelming floral smell.

He'd done this.

Paid dearly for hundreds of the blooms. And why? For Kit. To please Kit. In some misguided attempt to make up for a lifetime of wrongs.

Well, no matter what Beulah or even his own conscience told him, he was done being wrong.

Dammit, he was ready to live. Without Kit. He had Libby to consider and—

"Excuse me?" an older, graciously aged version

of Kit asked, hand on the sleeve of his dark suit. "But Travis Callahan? Is that you?"

Kit's mother. Could this day get any worse?

"Kit and I were just talking about you. She was telling me you're the one responsible for all of this," she said, waving her hands toward the opulent floral arrangements.

Looked like Chrissy had a big mouth. She was supposed to have told Kit the flowers had been on sale.

"Where is she?" he asked.

"In the pastor's parlor. It's just through that door and at the end of the hall if you'd like to pop in for a quick hug."

A quick hug?

It was all Travis could do not to choke.

How had it come to this? Kit's wedding day? It didn't even seem possible. No. Hell, no, he didn't want to see her. But he couldn't stop himself from taking the walk. At the very least, he should give her his last gift. Let her know how much he cared through deeds if not words.

"Travis," she said, startled when he entered without knocking.

Chrissy and Steph shared a bench at a mirrored vanity. The flower girl—Clara from the daycare—sat at their feet, brushing a doll's long hair. Her brother, Lincoln, was the ring bearer, but he must've been hanging with Levi.

Seeing Travis, Chrissy said, "Come on, Steph, Clara. Let's leave these two alone."

"Do I smell bad?" Travis quipped once they'd gone.

"Of course not," Kit said, her expression luminous and serene. She was happy. That was all he'd ever wanted, right? Rising from a beige leather wing chair, the sight of her took his breath away. "You're incredible," he said, swallowing the thick lump in his throat. "Levi's a lucky man."

"Th-thank you…" Was it just him or had she refused to meet his stare?

"I'm sure you're busy," he said, "doing all kinds of last-minute bride stuff, but I wanted to give you this." He fished in his jacket's chest pocket, withdrawing a sheath of papers.

"You've already given me—*us*—so much. The flowers are—well, they're spectacular but too much. Chrissy told me you insisted."

Casting her a faint smile, he shrugged.

"This is the last gift," he said, holding it out for her. "Promise."

She took the papers, opened the lengthwise fold. After taking a moment to digest the contents, her already bright eyes pooled with tears. "But…"

"There are legalities. Stacks of papers you'll need to sign. But for now, please know my sister's home and all the daycares are yours."

"Oh, Travis, no." As if they'd burst into flame, she shoved the papers at him. "No. I couldn't."

He shoved them right back. "You can and will. Marlene would've wanted it this way. Besides, now you and Levi will have a nice big home to start your family. And with me out of the way, I'm sure the daycares will run better than ever. Oh—and I've arranged for the house's front parlor to be redone however you want. Here's the contractor's card." He fished it from his suit coat pocket, handing it to her.

"But, Travis, I—" She gave him the oddest look. What was it? What had she almost said? In the past weeks, they'd shared so much. He'd thought he'd known her every nuance and touch. But not this. The woman standing before him was a stranger.

And so with the same cool politeness he would've shown a client's wife or daughter, Travis turned to leave the room.

He'd curved his fingers around the cold crystal doorknob when she said, "I'm wearing your earrings. See?"

Glancing over his shoulder, he found her drawing back her veil, showing him she spoke the truth. "A-and I wore my hair up—but loosely. I remember how you said it looked pretty that way."

"No," he said, marching toward her, knowing what he was about to do would be his undoing. "That's not what I said. *I* said if you wore it that way, Levi would enjoy taking it down. I never said a word about me, Kit."

"You did," she said with a teary-eyed nod. "I remember."

"I remember I was the only one sober. Could you maybe be thinking of what you wanted me to say?"

"No." A dazed expression marred her flawless

complexion. "No, I distinctly remember hearing that, because I—" She looked down, then up at him, piercing him with her wounded stare. "Because I…"

"You what, Kit? Say it. Just go ahead and say whatever's on your mind."

"I—I…" She was back to shaking her head, wringing her delicate beaded skirt.

And then something snapped in him. He couldn't have told even himself what was the cause, just that at that precise moment he'd decided to throw it all to the wind.

Everything.

His career, the Chicago penthouse.

He'd throw it all away for her.

"I love you," he said, breaking what little space was between them to drag her into his arms, plundering her mouth with his. Not caring if her lipstick smeared or if Levi noticed. Dammit, Kit belonged to him. She always had. He'd branded her all those years ago and now he was back to reclaim her. "God help me, I love you."

"I love you, too," she mewed against him, her lips still grazing his. "But—"

"No buts…" He pressed his fingers to her mouth. "Run away with me. We'll go out a back door. We'll pack up Libby and the dogs and run as far and fast as we can. We'll hide somewhere exotic with lots of palm trees and umbrella drinks. Lounging until all the rumors and gossip die down. I love you, Kit. Hell, I've always loved you. I just haven't had the sense God gave fleas. If I had, I would never have left you or IdaBelle Falls. I'd have stayed here with my grandma. I'd have been a part of something bigger than me. Better."

"But that's what you have in Chicago," she said. "Rose Industries employs thousands. You mean so much to so many people. You can't just hang out here. You deserve some perfect socialite who—"

He shut her up with more kisses. "Run away with me. Now. You know you want to. All you have to do is take the plunge. We'll worry about the consequences later."

Mind reeling, heart breaking, Kit couldn't begin to comprehend Travis's oh-so-tempting words.

He kissed her again. Hard, soft, dizzying in its wild splendor. "Marry me," he said. "Live with me. Have my babies and help me raise Libby."

Pulling away from him, she said, "I have to think. All of this is so—"

"I know it's sudden, gorgeous, but that's the beauty of the runaway-bride plan." He flashed her his trademark grin. The dead-sexy grin that never failed to turn her inside out with wanting. But did she truly love him or just want him? How was she supposed to know for sure? For that matter, how did she know he really loved her? They'd only been back together a short while. And even then, they weren't together as a couple but—she shook her head. "What you're proposing…it's madness. What about Levi? You don't love me. You love the idea of me, the—"

"Don't you dare," he said, pointing at her, shaking his finger. "Don't you dare presume to tell me what I feel. I once confessed I'm a coward when it comes to love, but dammit, Kit, I'm thinking maybe it's you who's the biggest coward of all. Either that or just plain stupid for not seeing that together we're the best damn thing to ever happen to each other."

Not bothering to hide her tears, she shook her head. "How do I know any of this is even real?"

"How do you know?" he asked with a raw laugh. *"How do you know?"* He slashed his fingers through his hair. "If you even have to ask, we obviously have nothing more to say."

With that, he turned and walked out the door.

Chapter Sixteen

"Kit-Kat," Kit's father said, patting the arm she'd looped through his, "your mother and I couldn't be more proud."

"Thank you," she said, eyes damp and not quite focused. Why had Travis even come? Why had he said all of those beautiful words if only to leave in a fury? Was he out there now? she wondered, scanning the chapel.

"Having a case of bridal jitters?"

Through a pinched grin she nodded. And she was cold. Despite the weight of twenty pounds of satin and tulle, she was so very cold.

After hugs and tears, Clara, Lincoln, Steph and Chrissy had preceded her down the aisle, and now, although standing next to her father, Kit felt alone in the world. Her best friend hated her. But then, what had he expected, throwing out asinine suggestions like her running away from the wedding she'd waited for her whole life?

Do you love him? Or do you just love the idea of having a wedding?

Shut up! she railed to her conscience. How many times did she have to tell herself Travis wasn't real. He was one of those fairy-tale princes she'd been so fond of as a kid.

Funny, 'cause his presence, his kiss, had seemed pretty real back in the dressing room.

She was no virgin, but after that kiss, she might as well have been, seeing how nothing she'd ever experienced with any man had equaled the power of that one heady moment.

"Daddy," she said, having a tough time breathing past the fine lace veil covering her face.

"Yes?"

"How did you know you wanted to marry Mom?"

"Seems like I always knew. Kind of the way you know with Levi. That's the beauty of love." He flashed her a reassuring smile. "It's loud."

Oh, it was loud all right, she thought as the organist launched into the bridal march. The place was filled to capacity, and Travis had gone overboard and ordered too many flowers. Not that she wasn't appreciative, but the floral scent—it was overwhelming. How would she ever make it to the end?

And all of a sudden, she wasn't just talking about the end of the aisle, where Levi stood looking ridiculously calm, but the end of her life. Yes, her father was right. Love was very loud.

Deafening.

And at the moment it was screaming for her to stop making the biggest mistake of her life. As much as Travis claimed to love her, she loved him a thousand times more.

But there stood Levi, and still she was walking, walking ever closer to a man she didn't know as well as she should. Toward a future she wanted no part of.

The cloying flowers and heat and stares—so many stares. *What am I doing? Run. Run!*

Internal radar told her Travis was long gone. Come to think of it, she hadn't seen Beulah or Libby or Frank either. Where was everyone?

"Almost there," her father whispered. "Smile. This day is all for you. Every single one of these people adores you, Kit-Kat."

Though she heard his sweet words, they didn't begin to register. All she heard was blood pounding in her ears.

Run. *Run!*

And then she'd reached the end of the aisle, and Chrissy and Steph were smiling and crying, and Levi was looking tall and strong and warm and friendly—like a big golden Lab. But was that what she wanted in a husband? Yes, but she also wanted so much more.

"Who gives this woman to this man?" Reverend Norgard asked.

"Her mother and I," her father said, lifting Kit's veil to plant a kiss to her cheek, then pass her along to the new man in her life.

The music had long since stopped, so why were her ears ringing? Like sirens wailing out a warning that what she was about to do was wrong. Even if Travis did leave again, she owed it to herself to at least find out if they had a chance. She loved Levi more as a brother and couldn't selfishly bind him to her this way.

"Lookin' good," he said with a friendly wink, skimming his hand along her forearm.

What had Travis said when he'd first seen her in her wedding finery? *You're incredible.*

She closed her eyes and swallowed hard.

"We are gathered here today…"

Run. Run. Run.

"…in holy matrimony. Marriage is a sacred act. One not to be entered into lightly or—"

"Stop," Kit wasn't sure if she'd said it aloud or in her head. "Stop."

"Kit?" her groom asked. "You feeling all right? Are you going to be sick?"

"No," she said with a vehement shake of her head. But she just might pass out!

"Then what's wrong?"

Somehow, amidst the candles' heat and the flowers' spell, she forced a deep breath. "I can't."

"What?"

"Levi, I thought this was what I wanted, but—"

"What?"

"You deserve more than me. A woman who loves you more than life itself."

He looked dazed and confused. "I don't get it. What're you saying?"

Passing her bouquet to Chrissy, she said to Levi and everyone else assembled, "I'm sorry. So very sorry. But there's not going to be a wedding today."

RUNNING DOWN THE CHAPEL steps, holding her skirts high in dazzling sun, Kit felt lighter than air.

Paul Sage, the hired driver, stood alongside his ancient white limo—the only one in town—used for both funerals and weddings. "Where's your groom?"

"We're going to get him," she said, climbing into the backseat. "Please—hurry."

He shot her a funny look but got behind the wheel. Easing down the privacy partition, he asked, "Not that it's any of my business, but where exactly does the groom reside?"

"Travis Callahan's place."

Paul made it in record time, but once Kit climbed out, hiking her long skirts up again to race onto the porch, the place felt stone-silent. Usually even if they were inside, the dogs yipped and yapped at the slightest sign of company. At the doorbell's peal, they would go haywire.

She waited ten minutes, her heart heavy.

A train rumbled by, but even that didn't bring the dog's barks or the baby's cries.

Where could Travis be? And why would the dogs be gone?

Unless…

We'll pack up Libby and the dogs and run as far and fast as we can.

Had he run without her? As light as she'd felt leaving the church, she now felt heavy. What had she done? What if he never came back? What if she never saw him again?

What if all this time he'd loved her? He'd just been too proud to admit it. Until at the chapel, when she'd thrown that love in his face.

Not caring if she dirtied her dress now, seeing how she obviously was never going to have need of it, Kit asked Paul to please take her home, where she started calling the airport, Travis's number in Chicago, his office, anywhere she thought he could be. When she hit a dead end with the last number on her list, Kit spent the remainder of her wedding day with her new best friends: Fritos, Doritos, Cheetos, Coke and Oreos.

Oh—and chocolate ice cream. Gallons and gallons of the healing stuff.

Then she heard a car crunch the gravel drive.

Great. Just great, she thought with a glance at her orange-junk-food-crumb-stained dress. Probably her parents. Or Chrissy and Steph. Or, the way her luck had been running, the enterprising T-shirt guy wanting permission to make a commemorative shirt celebrating the town's only runaway bride!

She peered out the window to find none of those intrusions but a black SUV.

"HURRY, FRANK, WE DON'T want to miss the plane."
Beulah tossed the last of her knee-high panty hose into
her good black suitcase—the one usually reserved for
church choir trips—then zipped it up tight.

Frank rolled his eyes. "It's a corporate jet. How
in the world would they take off without us?"

"I don't know," Beulah said, "but I sure-shootin'
don't want to tempt fate. Got your heating pad?"

"Yes, ma'am."

"How 'bout bringing that smelly cream you use
when your back gets to hurting?"

"Uh-huh."

"I still can't believe this. Flying all the way to
Chicago." She shook her head and whistled.

"You sure this is what you want to do?"

"You don't?" she asked with a snort, hefting her
bag from the bed onto the floor.

"Oh, now, I didn't say that. And while we're there,
I thought we might take in a few sights. I hear
Chicago has a mighty fine zoo."

"Libby will love that," Beulah said.

"We'll have to take her to some of those fancy
museums, too. She's young, but a little culture can't
hurt anything."

"Amen," Beulah said.

"Do you feel any more kindly toward Travis now
that he's made us this more than generous offer to
stay on with him like this, looking after Libby while
he's at the office?"

"I've always felt kindly toward him," she said

with a put-upon harrumph. "He's a good man. Obviously no good at wooing a pretty girl, but in time, with my assistance, he'll learn."

"Woman," Frank said with a shake of his head, "anyone ever tell you you're one peach shy of a bushel?"

THIS IS DUMB, TRAVIS mouthed to himself in the SUV, wondering what forces had led him back to this house. At the chapel Kit had given him a fairly clear answer. So why was he now back for more kicking?

Why? Because Harold Richmond at the IGA where Travis had stopped for diapers told him there'd been trouble down at the chapel. And God help him, though he'd never before been this gossipy, Travis had to know what that trouble had been.

If there was even a chance it concerned him, he *had* to know.

"Be right back," he said to the dogs, all three lolling on leather bench seats in air-conditioned comfort.

In the house, the curtain hanging over the window behind Kit's sofa shifted. Was she inside?

His mouth went dry.

Maybe this hadn't been such a great idea. She'd already turned him down once. Why would he have any reason to think she wouldn't do it aga—

"Travis…" she said, popping open the front door.

Her hair was a rummaged-though mess, her wedding gown as rumpled and stained as a messy toddler's birthday-party finery. Her makeup was ruined yet never had he seen her look more beautiful.

"Hey," he said past the lump in his throat.

"Hey." She laughed. Sniffled, using the backs of her hands to wipe her eyes. "Nice car."

He shrugged. "Seeing how I was never all that keen on the now-dead daycare van, I thought this might be a nice change of pace."

"You're too much," she said, lifting her voluminous skirt to dab her eyes.

"I like to think so."

She sniffled through tears.

"Anyway," he said at the foot of her porch stairs, shuffling his black leather shoes against the brick walk. "Heard there was trouble at the church."

"A little. Go figure. The bride just high-tailed it out of the chapel and ran off to find another man. But by the time she'd gotten to his house, I heard, he'd already left." Shrugging, she said, "'Course this is only hearsay. You know how folks in this town love to gossip."

"No way," he said, shoving his hands in his pockets while shaking his head. "This sweet town?"

"Don't trust the quaint appearance. This place is a regular hotbed of scandal."

"I'd've never guessed it."

She laughed, glanced across the yard toward his fancy ride. "Where are you going?"

"Me and the dogs thought we'd take a little road trip back up to Chicago. Take some time to think.

Beulah and Frank are flying to Chicago with Libby. They're going to stay with me, help her settle in."

"Sure," Kit said, fearful her heart just might pound out of her chest. "Sounds fun."

"Not really. But it beats the hell out of sticking around here, watching the woman I love marry another man."

"I, um…" She licked her lips, willing her rubbery knees not to buckle. "I heard there's a bride available, seeing how she bailed at the last minute at the altar. Want me to see if I can get her number for you?"

"I don't know. If she's the running type, what's to keep her from running from me?"

"Beats me," she said with an exaggerated sigh. "Guess it'd take a guy comfortable with risks to settle her down."

Nodding, looking down, then up, he said, "I have been known to take a corporate gamble or two in my day."

"Then who knows? Maybe she's the one for you."

"You think?"

Nodding, she practically hurtled herself off the porch and into his arms. "I love you. I love you more than life or breath or…life. I love you, I love you, I—"

He stopped her words with a hundred sparkling kisses, realizing that, with Kit in his arms, for the first time in his life all his questions had been answered. All he'd been seeking had been found.

Travis Callahan finally had a home and family that had nothing to do with a career or a place but a woman. An amazing woman he'd never again let go.

*Set in darkness beyond the ordinary world.
Passionate tales of life and death.
With characters' lives ruled by laws the
everyday world can't begin to imagine.*

Introducing NOCTURNE,
a spine-tingling new line from Silhouette Books.

The thrills and chills begin with
UNFORGIVEN
by Lindsay McKenna

Plucked from the depths of hell, former military sharpshooter Reno Manchahi was hired by the government to kill a thief, but he had a mission of his own. Descended from a family of shape-shifters, Reno vowed to get the revenge he'd thirsted for all these years. But his mission went awry when his target turned out to be a powerful seductress, Magdalena Calen Hernandez, who risked everything to battle a potent evil. Suddenly, Reno had to transform himself into a true hero and fight the enemy that threatened them all. He had to become a Warrior for the Light....

*Turn the page for a sneak preview of
UNFORGIVEN
by Lindsay McKenna.
On sale September 26,
wherever books are sold.*

Chapter 1

One shot...one kill.

The sixteen-pound sledgehammer came down with such fierce power that the granite boulder shattered instantly. A spray of glittering mica exploded into the air and sparkled momentarily around the man who wielded the tool as if it were a weapon. Sweat ran in rivulets down Reno Manchahi's drawn, intense face. Naked from the waist up, the hot July sun beating down on his back, he hefted the sledgehammer skyward once more. Muscles in his thick forearms leaped and biceps bulged. Even his breath was focused on the boulder. In his mind's eye, he pictured Army General Robert Hampton's fleshy, arrogant fifty-year-old features on the rock's surface. Air exploded from between his lips as he brought the avenging hammer down. The boulder pulverized beneath his funneled hatred.

One shot...one kill...

Nostrils flaring, he inhaled the dank, humid heat

and drew it deep into his massive lungs. Revenge allowed Reno to endure his imprisonment at a U.S. Navy brig near San Diego, California. Drops of sweat were flung in all directions as the crack of his sledgehammer claimed a third stone victim. Mouth taut, Reno moved to the next boulder.

The other prisoners in the stone yard gave him a wide berth. They always did. They instinctively felt his simmering hatred, the palpable revenge in his cinnamon-colored eyes, was more than skin-deep.

And they whispered he was different.

Reno enjoyed being a loner for good reason. He came from a medicine family of shape-shifters. But even this secret power had not protected him—or his family. His wife, Ilona, and his three-year-old daughter, Sarah, were dead. Murdered by Army General Hampton in their former home on USMC base in Camp Pendleton, California. Bitterness thrummed through Reno as he savagely pushed the toe of his scarred leather boot against several smaller pieces of gray granite that were in his way.

The sun beat down upon Manchahi's naked shoulders, grown dark red over time, shouting his half-Apache heritage. With his straight black hair grazing his thick shoulders, copper skin and broad face with high cheekbones, everyone knew he was Indian. When he'd first arrived at the brig, some of the prisoners taunted him and called him Geronimo. Something strange happened to Reno during his fight with the name-calling prisoners. Leaning down after he'd

won the scuffle, he'd snarled into each of their
bloodied faces that if they were going to call him
anything, they would call him *gan,* which was the
Apache word for *devil.*

His attackers had been shocked by the wounds on
their faces, the deep claw marks. Reno recalled
doubling his fist as they'd attacked him en masse. In
that split second, he'd gone into an altered state of
consciousness. In times of danger, he transformed
into a jaguar. A deep, growling sound had emitted
from his throat as he defended himself in the three-
against-one fracas. It all happened so fast that he
thought he had imagined it. He'd seen his hands
morph into a forearm and paw, claws extended. The
slashes left on the three men's faces after the fight
told him he'd begun to shape-shift. A fist made
bruises and swelling; not four perfect, deep claw
marks. Stunned and anxious, he hid the knowledge
of what else he was from these prisoners. Reno's
only defense was to make all the prisoners so damned
scared of him and remain a loner.

Alone. Yeah, he was alone, all right. The steel
hammer swept downward with hellish ferocity. As the
granite groaned in protest, Reno shut his eyes for just
a moment. Sweat dripped off his nose and square chin.

Straightening, he wiped his furrowed, wet brow
and looked into the pale blue sky. What got his attention was the startling cry of a red-tailed hawk as
it flew over the brig yard. Squinting, he watched the
bird. Reno could make out the rust-colored tail on the

hawk. As a kid growing up on the Apache reservation in Arizona, Reno knew that all animals that appeared before him were messengers.

Brother, what message do you bring me? Reno knew one had to ask in order to receive. Allowing the sledgehammer to drop to his side, he concentrated on the hawk who wheeled in tightening circles above him.

Freedom! the hawk cried in return.

Reno shook his head, his black hair moving against his broad, thickset shoulders. *Freedom? No way, Brother. No way.* Figuring that he was making up the hawk's shrill message, Reno turned away. Back to his rocks. Back to picturing Hampton's smug face.

Freedom!

* * * * *

Look for UNFORGIVEN
by Lindsay McKenna,
the spine-tingling launch title
from Silhouette Nocturne ™.
Available September 26,
wherever books are sold.

SAVE UP TO $30! SIGN UP TODAY!

The complete guide to your favorite
Harlequin®, Silhouette® and Love Inspired® books.

✓ Newsletter ABSOLUTELY FREE! No purchase necessary.

✓ Valuable coupons for future purchases of Harlequin,
Silhouette and Love Inspired books in every issue!

✓ Special excerpts & previews in each issue. Learn about all
the hottest titles before they arrive in stores.

✓ No hassle—mailed directly to your door!

✓ Comes complete with a handy shopping checklist
so you won't miss out on any titles.

- -

SIGN ME UP TO RECEIVE INSIDE ROMANCE
ABSOLUTELY FREE
(Please print clearly)

_____
Name

_____
Address

_____
City/Town   State/Province   Zip/Postal Code

(098 KKM EJL9)

Please mail this form to:
In the U.S.A.: Inside Romance, P.O. Box 9057, Buffalo, NY 14269-9057
In Canada: Inside Romance, P.O. Box 622, Fort Erie, ON L2A 5X3
OR visit http://www.eHarlequin.com/insideromance

IRNBPA06R   ® and ™ are trademarks owned and used by the trademark owner and/or its licensee.

SPECIAL EDITION™

Experience the "magic" of falling in love at Halloween with a new *Holiday Hearts* story!

UNDER HIS SPELL

by *KRISTIN HARDY*

October 2006

Bad-boy ski racer J. J. Cooper can get any woman he wants—except Lainie Trask. Lainie's grown up with him and vows that nothing he says or does will change her mind. But J.J.'s got his eye on Lainie, and when he moves into her neighborhood and into her life, she finds herself falling under his spell....

If you enjoyed what you just read,
then we've got an offer you can't resist!

Take 2 bestselling love stories FREE!

Plus get a FREE surprise gift!

Clip this page and mail it to Harlequin Reader Service®

IN U.S.A.	IN CANADA
3010 Walden Ave.	P.O. Box 609
P.O. Box 1867	Fort Erie, Ontario
Buffalo, N.Y. 14240-1867	L2A 5X3

YES! Please send me 2 free Harlequin American Romance® novels and my free surprise gift. After receiving them, if I don't wish to receive anymore, I can return the shipping statement marked cancel. If I don't cancel, I will receive 4 brand-new novels every month, before they're available in stores! In the U.S.A., bill me at the bargain price of $4.24 plus 25¢ shipping & handling per book and applicable sales tax, if any*. In Canada, bill me at the bargain price of $4.99 plus 25¢ shipping & handling per book and applicable taxes**. That's the complete price and a savings of at least 10% off the cover prices—what a great deal! I understand that accepting the 2 free books and gift places me under no obligation ever to buy any books. I can always return a shipment and cancel at any time. Even if I never buy another book from Harlequin, the 2 free books and gift are mine to keep forever.

154 HDN DZ7S
354 HDN DZ7T

Name	(PLEASE PRINT)	
Address	Apt.#	
City	State/Prov.	Zip/Postal Code

Not valid to current Harlequin American Romance® subscribers.

Want to try two free books from another series?
Call 1-800-873-8635 or visit www.morefreebooks.com.

* Terms and prices subject to change without notice. Sales tax applicable in N.Y.
** Canadian residents will be charged applicable provincial taxes and GST.
All orders subject to approval. Offer limited to one per household.
® are registered trademarks owned and used by the trademark owner and or its licensee.

AMER04R   ©2004 Harlequin Enterprises Limited